Elsie and the Lynx

DORA CAMPBELL

For Dolores Rose and all the Jersey City people.

One

My introduction to the rock-and-roll lifestyle began with a quiet pint.

Lila chose a pub called The White Mouse for my getting-over-Jules drink. The sign depicted a white mouse lifting a piece of yellow cheese, presumably good British cheddar or Stilton, to his mouth, his eyes bright and alert lest someone should deprive him of this treat. From what I could glimpse through the windows—a bar and a few tables—it looked more like someone's basement than a pub.

Any misgivings I'd had dissipated when we descended the stairs and opened the door. Warm air and the scent of beer assailed us. It wasn't a student pub, but a proper local, something I'd learned to recognize during my four months in England. Gas lamps cast a soft glow over the little room. In one corner, two old men in cloth caps chatted over pints; a stout woman with bouffant hair beamed behind the bar.

Here there was no evidence that it was 1973; indeed, apart from the barmaid's hair, there was no sign that the sixties had ever unfolded. It was the sort of place where nothing would happen, which was just what I needed.

"What'll it be, my loves?" the barmaid asked.

Lila ordered a half-pint of ale; I opted for half a lager. We chose a table far from the door.

"Thanks for coming out on a night like this," I said.

Lila shook her head quickly as she rolled a cigarette. "It's good to get out for a drink. Besides, I needed to get away from work and from Mrs. Barrymore."

"She means well. Still, it's kind of funny that we're twenty-three, and we have to make up stories about late nights at the library and postgraduate office. The nights I spent with Jules, I had to pretend I was visiting a friend in Birmingham."

"I think she guessed anyway." Lila flicked ash from her cigarette. "When I spend weekends with Harry, I always say I'm visiting my aunt."

"It helps being English. She'll believe your aunt stories, but she knows damn well my aunts are American."

Lila's grey eyes danced. "For once, I've hidden my deviance. Good thing the rent is low."

For a few minutes, we sipped in silence. This was supposed to be my getting-over-Jules drink, but I'd managed to talk about him.

I set down my glass. "I just wish I knew. Whether we're serious or not, whether we're together or not. For a month or so, around Christmas, I thought so. You know, he gave me the chocolates and the scarf. But he rings less often now, it's been two weeks since we've seen each other outside of university, and even at uni, he seems more distant. He's more animated when he talks to Belle."

"He's never broken up with me," I continued. "But then, I wonder if he has to. After all, we were never together. Not officially."

"That's hard."

"He always thought you didn't like him."

"Whenever I hear his name, I always think of Jules Verne."

"*Around the World in Eighty Days.*"

"Oh, more like *Twenty Thousand Leagues Under the Sea*," said Lila. "Let's get another drink." She rose from her chair. "Pints this time."

The two old men, now accompanied by two old women, were being served, so we had to wait at the bar. As we queued, I glanced at Lila. With her porcelain skin and dry humor, she seemed as English as the ale she drank, but her black hair with its severe bangs and kohl-rimmed eyes made her appear faintly exotic. When she wasn't at uni, she lived openly with Harry, a kind, long-haired engineer. She was gorgeous and brilliant, and she didn't care what people thought of her. If she weren't such a good friend, I'd be jealous of her.

No, I thought, studying her profile, no man would look twice at me when she was present. Next to her, I was drab with my frizzy, mousy brown hair and sallow skin even if I'd inherited my dad's dark blue eyes and my sister Maggie said she would kill for my figure. "It's not fair!" she'd exclaim. "You're a stick, but with curves for God's sake."

Behind me, the door opened, and cold air tickled my neck. Absently, I turned and saw two men about our age enter the pub. Both had long hair. One of them caught my eye and smiled. I found myself returning his smile before I turned back to the bar.

"The same again, my loves?" the barmaid was asking.

I felt a soft pressure on my elbow. "We'll get these."

I found myself looking up into warm dark eyes over high cheekbones. They belonged to the long-haired man who had smiled at me.

His hair was a rich brown and wavy, and he wore heavy bangs across his forehead.

"So, what'll you have?" he asked. The voice was northern, north of Manchester, that much I could tell.

"Lager." Back home, I'd never let a guy I didn't know buy me a drink. As my nana would say, it would give the Wrong Idea. Then again, back home, I didn't frequent bars. English pubs were different somehow. Nice women drank alone here.

"And your friend?"

Almost imperceptibly, Lila raised her eyebrows. "Ale."

"Three ales, one lager, then." He paid the barmaid and then turned to me. "Can we join you?"

I looked at Lila, and she lifted her shoulders slightly.

"Sure," I said.

And somehow, the four of us settled around the round table where Lila and I had been drinking alone. The other patrons' voices and the occasional clang of glasses receded as we spoke.

"I'm Alec," said the northerner. He gestured at his mate. "And this is Lucas. If you get him out of his pint, he can be quite conversable."

Shorter than his friend, Lucas had dark eyes that darted quickly around the room. Though he also had long hair, his hairline, I noticed, was already receding, and he wore a short, scruffy beard.

"And after a few pints, Alec starts to make sense," said Lucas. "And that's fucking terrifying." His accent was southern, near London, I guessed.

We laughed and introduced ourselves. And then somehow, Lucas was talking to Lila and Alec to me.

"You're obviously not from around here, Elsie," said Alec. "Canada?"

"States. And I thought my accent gave me away."

The dark eyes laughed above the pint glass. "I've learned to tread carefully with you lot. New York?"

"Close. Jersey City. Just across the Hudson."

"Like London and Reading."

"More or less."

"And what brings you to Manchester, Elsie?"

"A course. I'm doing a master's in English at Manchester Uni."

"Why England and Manchester in particular?"

I hesitated. I always felt funny talking to English people about my feelings for their country; the rush of sentiment always seemed so un-English.

"I guess I've always been drawn to your country—even as a child." I winced. I sounded like an earnest little girl with my shy American voice. "I loved English books; I wanted to be English. So when I had an opportunity to study in England, I seized it, and Manchester had a good reputation for seventeenth-century poetry."

To my surprise, Alec was listening to me thoughtfully. "So Donne and Rochester and Marvell and Herrick," he said.

"You know them?" I asked. Outside of English teachers and professors, few people could rattle off four seventeenth-century poets.

"I liked English at school," he replied. "I did well though I didn't go on to university." He looked down briefly.

It was obviously a sore point. I decided to change the subject. "What do you do now, Alec?" I asked.

"I play guitar," he said.

"What sort of music?" I asked.

He seemed taken aback. Did he expect me to recognize him? "Pop, rock. I'm in a band called Serval."

"I've heard of it," I said politely. I had, too. I just couldn't remember where.

A smile hovered over his mouth and eyes. They were velvety eyes, I thought. Then I reprimanded myself for such a ridiculous observation.

"We're playing a gig at the Free Trade Hall tomorrow."

"That's it!" I said. "I saw a poster in the center earlier."

He laughed. "Well, I'm glad we were that memorable anyhow."

"Is Lucas in the band?"

"Not Serval, no. He's part of the crew. But he's a musician, a damn good bassist and mandolin player. We have a little side project together."

"What sort of music do you play?"

"Bluesier stuff. When we get a chance, that is."

"Do you mean you don't have time?"

Alec shook his head. "Between touring, writing, and rehearsing, Serval eats up most of my time."

"Time, ladies and gentlemen," called the woman behind the bar.

"It's not even eleven!" said Lila.

"Oh, well, I guess we can't outrage Mrs. Barrymore if we go home early," I said.

Alec's eyes twinkled. "Mrs. Barrymore?"

"Our landlady."

"A fire-breathing dragon?"

"No, just someone who's unaware the last twenty years have happened. She holds us to a strict curfew: if we want to stay out past ten, we have to say we're working late at uni."

The dark eyes grew merrier. "And if you don't come home until morning?"

"Then we'd better be visiting our aunts."

Alec laughed and drained his glass. He leaned toward me, and I smelled ale and his leather jacket, but there was something else behind it, something musky. Without thinking, I bent my head toward it.

He breath was inches from my ear. I held mine. "The night's young, and I wouldn't mind another drink. We could always order a bottle of champagne at my hotel if you'd like to come back."

I sat bolt upright. "No, thank you, I have to go to uni tomorrow." My voice sounded high-pitched and nervous, like a little girl's.

He bit back a chuckle. "Then Lucas and I will bid you farewell. As I said before, we're playing at the Free Trade Hall tomorrow. If you and your friend— Linda—want to come, there'll be tickets for you there. Just ask at the box office."

He wanted to see me again? A frizzy-haired little girl who'd just rebuffed him?

"Her name is Lila," I said. "But thanks."

He smiled, we said our goodbyes, and he and Lucas disappeared into the night.

"I was invited back to the hotel for champagne," I announced as Lila and I walked through the rain past silent brick buildings.

"That was quick." Lila was dry.

"How was his friend?"

"He's a nice bloke; he told me right away he was going out with an art student."

"Did he tell you what they do for work?"

"Just that he's a roadie for Alec's band."

"Which is Serval. They're playing at the Free Trade Hall tomorrow. Apparently, there'll be tickets at the box office for us."

"As I said, that is quick."

"Oh, it's nothing like that," I said. "He was probably just bored. And who knows if he'll even remember about the tickets. He's probably pulling someone else right now. Isn't that what rock stars do?"

Lila shrugged. "Well, we should go if only to hear some live music for free. And Alec seems better than Jules Vernon anyway."

For a second, I halted. Jules was the reason we had visited The White Mouse, after all. Alec and Lucas had been a distraction, a story to tell Maggie the next time we talked.

Raindrops pelted my forehead, but I hardly noticed as we turned into the street where Mrs. Barrymore lived in her brick rowhouse.

Two

In the drab light of morning, our breakfast illuminated by the single bulb above Mrs. Barrymore's dining room table, it was hard to believe that a pub called The White Mouse and a band called Serval existed, much less that we had been invited to see the latter in concert

"You young ladies were very late at the university last night," said Mrs. Barrymore. The smell of fried eggs and potatoes wafted up to me as she spooned them onto my plate.

"They must be very busy with their studies," said Ralph Taylor. A barrister's clerk, he would have been quite nice-looking if his sandy hair had not been cut in a bowl-shape. His left eyebrow often twitched, the result, perhaps, of being both Mrs. Barrymore's boarder and her nephew.

"Mr. Singh is a law student, and his studies never keep him out late." Triumphantly, Mrs. Barrymore assumed her seat the end of the table and took a sip of coffee. She was tall and big-boned, and with her thick glasses and greying brown curls, which were permed and set at regular intervals, she looked like a sterner version of Mary Whitehouse, the moral crusader.

Over his eggs, Ravi Singh grinned at Mrs. Barrymore.

"But I can bring most of my lawbooks home, Mrs. Barrymore. Besides, law is not such a big field as Egyptology or English literature; it is only natural Miss Hedges and Miss Farrell should put in long hours at the library and postgraduate office."

Beneath her bottle glasses, Mrs. Barrymore's green eyes softened.

"You're a kind young man, Mr. Singh, as well as clean and civil," she said.

I caught Lila's eye. Mrs. Barrymore always described Ravi as clean and polite, both when she referred to him and when she addressed him directly. Thus, she assured him, the world, and herself she harbored no prejudice against Indians.

"I suppose you young ladies will be in early tonight after last night's exertions," said Mrs. Barrymore with some dignity.

"Probably not," replied Lila, buttering a piece of toast. "I'm in the middle of some research about cat mummification."

"Heathen nonsense," Mrs. Barrymore murmured.

That meant Lila planned to attend the concert. I wasn't even sure I wanted to go. But I had to support her.

"And I'm researching Royalist poetry," I said.

"Their research is so very interesting," said Ravi. "Truly I am lucky to lodge with two such scholarly ladies."

"Hmph," said Mrs. Barrymore. "Well, far be it from me to keep students from their studies." She sipped her coffee.

"However useless they may be," she muttered.

I resisted the urge to catch Lila's eye. I did smile at Ravi, who nodded and beamed in return.

"It was good of Ralph and Ravi to stick up for us," I said to Lila as we walked to campus together. "Poor Ralph being Mrs. Barrymore's nephew and Ravi being her favorite foreigner. Though I don't know exactly why I feel sorry for them; they get to stay out a whole hour later than we do. Of course, I've never seen either of them stay out until eleven, much less past it."

"Perhaps they have a secret life."

"Yes, they sneak out their bedroom windows and go to clubs when Mrs. Barrymore's asleep. Speaking of secret lives, I've rather gone off the concert."

"Oh?"

"Well, it's not as though I'm that familiar with the music, and who knows if the tickets will be there, and even if they are, I'll feel like a groupie or something."

"I don't think groupies usually get free tickets to shows," said Lila dryly.

"N-no. I guess I'd just feel conspicuous; it'll look like I'm chasing Alec."

"Not necessarily. Bands probably have tickets set aside for friends or family. The people in the box office might just assume you're his sister or something."

"His long-lost American sister."

Lila smiled. "Well, it'll be free music anyway. If we really hate it, we can just leave."

I had a lecture that morning about parliamentary poets during the English Civil War. Dr. Timothy Burgess, the lecturer, wore a tweed coat that was always topped with a veneer of chalk dust. He attempted to comb his fine white hair over the great gaping bald spot on his crown, but by the middle of lectures, his combover flapped like a white feather. This, coupled with his thick Glaswegian accent, made him a figure of fun to many students. He also rambled in lectures, so he was a caricature of the absent-minded professor.

But I liked Dr. Burgess. He was a fount of knowledge about the seventeenth century and its literature, and though his lectures were always full of digressions about minor poets and courtiers and religious sects, I always relished these forays into the era. And so, for an hour and half, I traveled back to the 1640s with a dusty Glaswegian guide.

After the lecture, I had a cup of tea in the English postgraduate office, a cozy, rather shabby room on the third floor of the Arts Building Extension. It boasted a tea kettle, some mismatched teacups and saucers, and a few odd pieces of lounge furniture that appeared as if they had been donated by our lecturers a couple decades earlier. It was equipped with a few desks, but I seldom saw anyone using them.

Larry Randall and Clara Brooks joined me. They, too, had attended the lecture.

"That was interesting, I thought," said Larry in his deep, BBC voice. Despite its depth, his voice had a certain hesitancy. Tall and thin, he stooped as if to hide his height.

Clara nodded. "'Twas." From Newcastle, she wore her auburn hair short and favored trousers and tweed sport coats.

"For all that people laugh at Tim, I like his lectures," I said.

"What's this?" asked a familiar voice.

Jules Vernon and Belle Hocks stepped into the office. Jules wore the blue pullover that made his eyes appear bluer still. Belle sported a brown suede miniskirt, a green sweater, and high brown boots. She tossed her waist-length red hair, and the smile frozen on her lips struck me as faintly triumphant.

"We just attended Tim's lecture on parliamentary poets during the English Civil War," I said. "It was interesting." Despite my efforts, there was a slight note of defiance in my voice. Jules had always been dismissive of my research.

Jules smirked. "Ah, Tim, all tweed and chalk dust like something from a minor public school seventy years ago. He probably dines on tinned puddings in his lodging."

"He is the absent-minded professor," I said. "But he does know a great deal about the seventeenth century."

"The question is, does he know about anything else?"

Belle alone laughed at this.

"Well, I'm glad he's at Manchester," I said. "I came here to immerse myself in that period."

This time, the smirk was confined to Jules's eyes. "Oh, yes, your affection for the metaphysical poets and the Civil War."

"I don't know why people get stuck on classroom stuff when there's been so much—innovation—in the last thirty years," said Belle. "I think being stuck in the past says something about their psyche." Once again, she tossed her hair.

I was tempted to ask what diagnosis an interest in seventeenth-century poetry suggested compared to that, say, demonstrated by a passion for Restoration drama.

Clara lit the cigarette she'd been rolling. "Well, we're all here to do a degree in English literature—isn't that the bloody point?" she said. "I'll write my dissertation about women novelists in the 1860s, but I want to soak up as much knowledge as I can here whilst I'm here, whether it's Tim's lectures about Civil War poets or Scott's about medieval drama. If I'm going to teach, I damn well want to know what I'm talking about."

Larry nodded while Jules and Belle smiled as though Clara had been prattling on about Father Christmas.

"Anyone got anything on for the weekend?" Larry asked. It was like him to make peace by changing the subject.

"Work," Clara sighed.

"Some live jazz, I think," said Jules thoughtfully. I saw him catch Belle's eye, the way he used to do when we had plans.

"You know, I suspect we're going to the same gig," she said. Out of the corner of her eye, she shot a look at me.

My cheeks grew hot. Wasn't it enough that she had Jules? Did she have to gloat about it?

"What are you doing, Larry?" I asked as calmly as I could.

"Work. Though Rogers and I might grab a curry once she gets off her shift at the hospital."

I was charmed by how Larry referred to his wife by her maiden name. It was very British.

"What about you, Elsie?" asked Belle as she rolled a cigarette. "Sending postcards home and volunteering at the jumble sale?" I had once helped Mrs. Barrymore at her church's jumble sale, and Belle would never let me forget it. She smirked as she inserted the cigarette in her mouth.

"Not this weekend," I replied. "Lila and I are going to a concert. Serval at the Free Trade Hall." Somehow, I had decided to go.

Belle almost choked on her fag. "Surely, that's a little square for you?" she tittered. "All those screaming girls and the guys in leather?"

"I didn't know you liked rock music, Belle."

She exhaled smoke. "I prefer jazz." She bloody well would.

"Well, I prefer rock," I said. "I don't know that much about Serval, but I can't resist free concert tickets." I rose from the settee, lingering just long enough to register the astonishment on Belle's and Jules's faces. I had exhausted my wit, and I didn't feel like explaining how we had procured our free tickets. If we had procured them.

Lila laughed when I recounted the story on our way to the concert that evening.

"Good," she said. "Belle's always bluffing. She'll do anything to obscure her lack of knowledge, even if it's putting down someone else's interests. And you've given Jules something to think about."

"I just intimated we had free tickets."

"But that's enough, isn't it? He doesn't know how we got them or who gave them to us. He does know you have a life outside of him and the English postgrad office."

"Do I?"

"Absolutely. You're a brilliant writer and scholar, and a well-known guitarist has invited you to see his show."

It was nice to hear her say it. It just sounded as though she were talking about someone far more interesting and alluring than I.

The Free Trade Hall was a two-story sandstone building lined by arched entranceways. Outside, there was a long queue. And our fellow concertgoers were, I noted, much as Belle had predicted, a collection of girls rather younger than ourselves and men in leather jackets.

Lila pointed. "There are two queues. One for people buying tickets and one for those who already have them."

We joined the latter, which moved quickly. Soon, we were at the ticket office. A blond with blue eyeshadow chewed gum at us.

Here went nothing.

"Tickets were being held for us? I'm Elsie, and this is Lila?" I sounded about fourteen.

The blond snapped her gum and handed them over. I picked them up casually as though I were accustomed to being admitted to shows for free. I caught Lila's eye, and she smiled slightly.

Our seats were about two-thirds of the way toward the front beside an exit door. Should there be an emergency, we should be able to leave in a hurry. Now there was a thought worthy of a rock star.

The opening band played a few songs, mostly Who and Pink Floyd and Led Zeppelin and Deep Purple covers and an original song that seemed a pretext for the keyboardist to play a long, complicated solo. I felt sorry for them, so I applauded with more energy than I felt.

When the opening band left the stage, the audience—at least, the younger, female part of it—started screaming. Howling, really.

"And I thought servals were a wild cat," Lila shouted in my ear. "But that sounds more like a wolf howl."

Then Serval came on stage. I recognized the singer with his wavy blond hair from the poster and Alec, of course, from The White Mouse. The bassist had a dark beard and the drummer a moustache.

And they could play. I recognized a couple songs from the radio; they had penetrated even my world of seventeenth-century poetry and dusty library books and calls home and Mrs. Barrymore's teas. But I recognized that the truly great songs, the ones that had the guys applauding as fiercely as the mini-skirted girls, were the one I had never heard before. Alec could really play, I noted with some pride. Then I wondered what right I had to be proud of him.

The band left the stage, there was deafening applause and more howling and stomping from the balcony above us, and the band returned. They played another song, a radio hit. Then they strode off the stage again, and fans started streaming out of the hall.

We decided it would be easier to let the others leave first, so we stood by our seats.

"Lila! Elsie!" someone shouted.

Two men in denim jackets waved frantically as they pushed through the crowd toward us. At first, I didn't recognize them. Then I noticed the bowl haircut.

"We didn't know you were coming," said Ralph when they finally stood in front of us.

"Well, we couldn't exactly be honest with Mrs. Barrymore," replied Lila.

Eyes downcast, Ralph shrugged. She was his aunt after all.

"Anyhow, it is very pleasant that we are all here together," said Ravi. "Would you ladies like a drink? There is a very nice pub just around the corner."

I opened my mouth to accept the invitation, but before I could reply, the side door opened. Suddenly, one of the largest men I had ever seen stood in front of us. He must have been almost seven feet tall, and his shoulders were nearly as broad as he was tall.

"Elsie? Lisa?" he asked in a surprisingly light Irish voice.

I repressed a giggle. "She's Lila," I said.

"Anyway, you're both invited to the afterparty. There's a car just outside." He pointed to the door.

My eyes flitted to Lila. She lifted her eyebrows slightly: she was leaving it up to me.

"Okay, thank you," I said to the tall man.

"We'll get that drink another time," Lila told our fellow boarders. Their eyes were large, and Ralph's eyebrow twitched.

"Sorry," I said over my shoulder. I didn't want to be rude, and at any other time, a drink with our fellow lodgers would have been pleasant. But I had been invited to a concert afterparty, and I wasn't about to pass up the opportunity. It would be something to tell my sister Maggie and my friends back home.

As we followed the giant through the side door, I wondered which was more surreal: seeing Ralph and Ravi at a rock concert or being summoned to a party after the same show.

A white limousine idled in the side street outside the hall. Beside it, a man stood smoking a cigarette. It was Lucas, the roadie who had accompanied Alec at The White Mouse the night before. When he saw us, his brow furrowed.

"Good evening, Lila, Elsie. The party's at the Piccadilly Hotel. Alec and the others will be along soon." Grimly, he opened the limo's back door.

Thanking him, we climbed into the vehicle. As we drove away, I wondered why he looked so miserable. We'd all gotten along so well the night before.

Three

Lucas sat up front beside the driver. For a few minutes, he was silent. Then he faced us, smiling tightly.

"Did you enjoy the show?" he asked. He emitted the words grudgingly as if uttering them cost him a great deal of energy.

"Yes!" I replied with more animation than I felt. "They're very talented."

"Hmph."

"They're good," said Lila in the more measured tone I wished I had employed.

"Hmm."

Really, he was beginning to sound like our grumpy grandpa. Had I said anything to offend him? I decided to show an interest in him.

"Alec says you play in a band together," I said.

"Yes, our little side project. Very sidelined of late."

Clearly, I'd done nothing to dispel his mood.

"I'm sorry," I said. "Sorry you've not had more time for it, that is. I do hope you have more time to practice in the future."

"Thank you." He paused. "So you're doing a master's in English?"

"Yes. I came to Manchester to study seventeenth-century poetry."

"Donne and Herrick and Rochester."

"Yes." Here was someone else outside my world who could rattle off seventeenth-century poets. I wouldn't have imagined that a rock musician, let alone a roadie, would be aware of these long-dead versifiers.

In the front seat, Lucas nodded. "It's nice to know they're not neglected."

"You like poetry."

"Yes, although my interest is in the late Victorian novel. I'm halfway through a degree, and I'd like to do my dissertation on Thomas Hardy if I ever get my arse back to uni. Here we are. The Piccadilly Hotel."

I'd walked by the Piccadilly countless times during my sojourn in Manchester, and I knew it was considered the city's premier hotel. Still, it had never appealed to me. With its blocky shape and its rows of windows, it looked like a larger version of the Arts Building Extension crouching over the city center.

But, of course, I had never imagined that I would attend a party there.

As Lila and I climbed out of the limo, I felt woefully underdressed. True, we were both in flared jeans, sweaters, or jumpers as the English called them, and coats, but whereas Lila always looked like Cleopatra transported to the seventies, I perpetually appeared as though I'd dressed for the lecture hall and then ended up someplace else. Then again, I had no idea how people dressed at these events. The band wasn't exactly swishy in their leather and denim; it was hardly fair to expect us to dress up.

And yet, the Piccadilly's bar held some girls in silk minidresses and fur stoles. They were younger than we were, and Lucas did not introduce us to them. They chatted in groups with some guys—other roadies, I suspected. Lucas led us to the bar and got us our drinks, the usual ale and lager. As he ordered our drinks, I studied our fellow guests discreetly. Maggie would want to hear every detail when I recounted the story later.

Once we were served, he stood grimly by us, sipping his own pint. When he offered us cigarettes and I said I didn't smoke, he frowned again as though I had confirmed his suspicions. Perhaps I was too square for the afterparty.

Then the opening band and Serval arrived. No doubt they had been transported in limos of their own. The circle of denim-clad guys and silk and fur-garbed girls mobbed the band. Lucas, Lila, and I remained by the bar.

The band eventually moved toward the bar, and I had the satisfaction of seeing Alec spot and approach me. His dark eyes met mine, and I smiled a welcome. For a moment, there was no one else in the room but us.

"I'm glad you've come, Elsie," he said in his rough northern voice. He leaned forward, and his hand grazed my hip. The warmth of his touch lingered after he'd withdrawn his hand.

"Thank you for inviting us," I said. Even as I spoke, I was aware of the incongruity of my prim voice at a concert afterparty.

Again, his eyes danced as he bit his lip.

"Hey, Lucas, Linda, you all right," he said.

Lucas merely scowled. Lila raised her eyebrows. "Yes, except that I've turned into Lila."

"Oh, sorry." There was something endearingly sheepish about his smile with his slightly crooked bottom teeth.

Then he turned back to me. "Has Lucas been looking after you and your friend?"

I nodded. "Yes, he's been very kind."

"So he's been earning his keep."

Lucas made a face, something between a sneer and a snarl. I decided to make peace by changing the subject.

"And thank you for inviting us to the concert. We enjoyed it." I sounded like a well-brought up little girl.

This time, Alec laughed outright. "Well, we try our best."

Suddenly, the crowd of band members and girls was upon us. I saw the singer's eyes alight on Lila, and though a blond girl had an arm through his, he extricated himself from her.

"Alec, introduce us to your friends," he said.

"Greg, Elsie and Lila, Elsie and Lila, Greg."

"Well met, Elsie," said Greg though he didn't look at me. Instead, he stepped toward Lila and put an arm around her. For a moment, they made quite a striking pair—him with his wavy fair hair and square-jawed face and Lila with her black hair and porcelain skin.

"I'm glad you came, Lila, my dear," he said. "I hope we'll get to know each other better."

Deftly, she sidestepped his arm. "Just tell us where we can get another drink."

His green eyes almost burst from his face.

"The bar," he said, gesturing feebly with one finger. "There."

It was clear few women had rebuffed him. Maggie would enjoy this anecdote.

Lucas and Lila stepped toward the bar, while I stood beside Alec. His fingers rested lightly on my hip, teasingly proprietary. I couldn't help feeling flattered that he had chosen me to accompany him to this party.

The blond Greg had spurned for Lila was ready to forgive him. She stepped forward and stroked his arm. After a moment, he smiled down at her. She returned his smile eagerly, and I was sorry for her.

The bearded bassist was addressing two blond girls. "I've been playing bass thirteen, fourteen years—half my life, really," he said.

His audience nodded earnestly as though all of this were of intense interest to them.

"Well, I don't play any instruments, but I have a special feeling for music," said one of the girls. "I can hear it in my head."

Lucas and Lila had rejoined us.

"And all this time, I've been calling it earworm," Lila murmured.

It was one of the most absurd statements I had ever heard. Lila's eyes met mine, and I broke into giggles.

"Time for another drink," Alec said, but instead of heading to the bar, he steered me to a small alcove off the room.

His dark eyes shone in the dimly lit space.

"If you can't keep a straight face or a civil tongue in your head, there's no use for it," he said.

He pulled me toward him, and his lips were on mine. There was nothing in the world but his breath, all hot ale, and the hands that drew me nearer to him.

When our lips parted, his mouth strayed to my neck, his stubble grazing my skin. I made a small sound, and he kissed my neck again.

I stepped closer, and his arms tightened around my shoulders. My head rested against his leather jacket. There was the smell of leather and musk I remembered from the night before. I'd never been this drawn to any man before.

Then his breath was warm on my ear. "We could get a bottle of champagne if you want to move the party upstairs," he said huskily.

I froze. This was why we'd been invited to the party. In me, Alec saw an easy, naïve conquest, just as Jules had. I was a fool not to have anticipated it, especially after the previous night.

"I'm sorry; I must be going," I said, pulling away from him. "I have to get up early tomorrow."

"I'll get you a cab—"

"We can pay our own way." I winced. It was the sort of dialogue an earnest high school student would write. "Anyway, thanks for the concert and the drink."

"Elsie—"

But I didn't wait to hear what he was going to say. Instead, I hastened into the bar and quickly found Lila. Once again, she and Lucas had separated themselves from the main group. At my approach, she raised her eyebrows almost imperceptibly.

"I'm really tired," I said, more for Lucas's benefit than anything. "I'm ready to go home if you are."

We said goodbye to Lucas and reentered the January night. For a moment, I regretted not allowing Alec to summon a cab for us. Then, I remembered I was a liberated woman. I was studying for a master's in another country; I'd earned a Marshall Scholarship, for God's sake. I was practically obligated to pay my own taxi fares, especially when the man offering to pay had what my nana would call the Wrong Idea.

Not far from the hotel, we hailed a cab. We were quiet on the way home. We would find some other time to discuss the evening. I certainly didn't want the driver to hear the whole messy story. At this point, I wasn't even sure I wanted to tell my sister about our adventure.

"Oh, God," I cried. "Ralph and Ravi know where we went. They'll tell Mrs. Barrymore."

Four

Mrs. Barrymore served breakfast at seven on weekends and weekdays alike. She didn't hold with us cooking for ourselves. "I don't need you meddling in my kitchen any more than you need me riffling through your desks," she'd announced when we'd moved in. Even making toast constituted meddling as Lila had discovered during our first week in the house. So if we wanted to eat in the mornings, we had to present ourselves at Mrs. Barrymore's dining room table at seven. Five minutes before seven to be exact.

The morning after the concert, I made it. Lila didn't. I was an incurably early riser—my body willed me to get up at six no matter how late I'd been out. Not that we'd stayed out late, really. We'd entered the house a little past midnight, sneaking upstairs as stealthily as possible.

I slid onto my chair, murmuring a good morning to Ravi, Ralph, and Mrs. Barrymore. Or rather to Mr. Singh, Mr. Taylor, and Mrs. Barrymore since our landlady didn't hold with Christian names.

I didn't dare make eye contact with Ralph or Ravi.

"How did your research go, Miss Farrell?" asked Ralph.

"Fine, thanks." Was this his attempt at sarcasm?

"Yes, it was so nice to see you and Miss Hedges at the library last night," said Ravi, smiling. "How pleasant it was to put aside my lawbooks and see your friendly and studious faces."

"It – it was lovely to see you as well," I faltered.

"Of course, I was rather envious of you and Miss Hedges with your postgraduate offices. You were able to carry on studying long after I went home. And then, on my return, who should I happen to meet but Mr. Taylor, who was also heading home after a long evening of work."

Swallowing a mouthful of sausage, Ralph nodded. "Mr. Tompkins kept me very late working on a brief."

Mrs. Barrymore shook her head. "Well, you're a hardworking lot, I'll say that much. If Miss Hedges should like some tea and toast when she rises, I won't say no to her. Though what could interest her about cat mummification I can't tell."

Mrs. Barrymore, who cordially disliked cats, mummies, and probably Egyptians, shuddered and sipped her coffee.

"Thank you," I mouthed to Ralph and Ravi when she returned to the kitchen to fetch more toast.

They smiled, Ralph rather shyly, and for the first time, I realized they were not merely harmless fellow lodgers, but allies.

Later that afternoon, long after Lila had enjoyed her ration of toast and tea, Mrs. Barrymore's telephone rang. It was my mom calling from the States, or Jersey City, as I preferred to think of it.

"Hi, honey, is this a good time to talk?" she asked.

"Mrs. Barrymore's out doing her weekly shop, so yes, I can talk."

I felt faintly deviant, curled up on Mrs. Barrymore's stiff green sofa though why I should feel so I didn't know. My parents were paying for the call, I didn't expect to discuss anything scandalous, and I was talking to my mom after all. But Mrs. Barrymore specialized in making adults feel like naughty children.

There was so much to discuss: Maggie and her two-year-old son Patrick, who was now talking up a storm, our cat Emily and dog Nellie, the mystery my mom was reading, and a new recipe for crumb cake she'd found in *Good Housekeeping*. In turn, I told her about my studies.

"Oh, and Lila and I went to a concert last night," I said.

"With Jules?" A stiffness had crept into her voice.

"No, just Lila. Jules and I are through." I was amazed at how calmly I delivered the news.

"Oh, honey. Are you okay?"

"I'm fine, Mom. It had run its course, and I think it's for the best." It was hard to believe Lila had had to console me by taking me out for a drink just a few days earlier.

Mom was silent. She obviously expected some explanation.

"He's taken up with Belle. You know, that redhead I told you about."

"Oh, her." She sniffed. "Anyway, I wish I could hug you."

"Me, too, but I'm fine, Mom. Really. A couple days ago, I was pretty cut up as the Brits say. But now it seems as though—the right thing happened."

"I'm so glad to hear you say that. But if you need to talk, you can call me anytime, day or night. You can call collect; your father won't mind."

"Thank you." Collect calls were expensive for people like my parents. Even our monthly phone calls were a luxury for them.

Next, I talked to my nana, who lived with my parents. Before my mom handed the phone to her, she whispered, "She's not going out with Jules anymore."

"Oh?" said Nana with great interest and concern.

When Nana got on the phone, she was as warm and interested as my mom had been. She was very impressed with my Marshall Scholarship and with me generally. She wanted to hear all about my English university and English friends and English life. She was particularly curious about the concert.

"What sort of music did this band play, dear?" she asked.

"Rock."

"Are they favorites of you and your friend?"

"Well, we really didn't know too much about them until last night. The night before, someone gave us free tickets at a pub, so we went."

"That's nice, dear. You and your friend had a free outing, and I'm sure it made the group feel good to have people attend their shows. Entertainers live to perform, you know."

I bit my lip. I wondered how Alec would react to Nana's remark. I imagined his dark eyes filled with laughter.

I spoke to my dad last. We talked only a few minutes.

"Well, you know I'm not much at talking on the phone," he said gruffly. "But I love you, and your mother and I miss you more than you know."

The lump in my throat lingered long after I hung up. I stared at Mrs. Barrymore's anemic watercolor prints of the British coast. I was fulfilling a lifelong dream of studying and living in England. I was having, on the whole, a wonderful time, and yet I had so much waiting for me on the other side of the ocean. And I knew I could call Maggie any time, day or night, and regardless of whether she was changing Patrick's diapers or ironing George's shirts, she would be all ears.

I had to be one of the luckiest women on either side of the Atlantic.

The phone rang. "Hello," I said jauntily. Even though it was probably one of Mrs. Barrymore's church friends, I somehow expected to hear Maggie's voice, warm and teasing.

But the voice that answered me was cool, male, and British. "Elsie? Is that you?"

Who did he think it was? Did Mrs. Barrymore have other American lodgers?

"Hello, Jules," I said. "You all right?"

"For the most part. You see, I've run into something with my research, and I want your opinion on it. We could get a cup of tea tomorrow or a curry. Your choice."

"I don't why I said yes," I said as I buttoned my coat in the foyer the next day. "I expect he took me by surprise."

Lila shrugged. "Well, at least you'll get a cup of tea out of it. Make him buy you a pastry or something."

"They do have nice cakes at Meng and Ecker. And if Mrs. Barrymore comes back from church while I'm out, can you tell her I'm meeting a friend for tea?"

"Of course."

As I stepped out the door, she called, "Make him grovel."

I couldn't quite imagine myself making any man grovel, but her words buoyed me forward even as the damp wind conspired to drive me indoors. Lila, I knew, was on my side, not that I'd ever doubted it.

Still, as I passed the rowhouses on our street and began advancing toward the center, I felt a heaviness in my stomach as though I were heading to my execution rather than a mere meeting at a café.

Only a few days earlier, Jules's invitation would have elated me. Today, I found myself dreading the rendezvous. What had changed exactly?

Of course, just two days earlier, he had publicly made plans with Belle. Was he trying to get me back because something had gone wrong with her? Was he indicating that he wanted to remain friends? Or maybe he just wanted my opinion on his dissertation though why he should suddenly value my advice when he'd never done anything of the kind while we were seeing each other was beyond me.

Meng and Ecker was located in St. Ann's Passage, the arcade between King Street and St. Ann's Square. Before I entered the café, I paused to admire the display of pastries and wedding cakes in the window. Then I realized I was stalling for time.

Upstairs, Jules occupied a table in the corner. He wore a corduroy blazer over another blue pullover that made his blue eyes appear bluer still. With his regular features and dark blond hair, he was good-looking even if his eyes were a little too close set and even if there was a sharpness about his features that prevented him from being absolutely handsome. In the autumn, soon after the course began, I had been somewhat shy around him. That seemed ages ago now.

He stood when he saw me.

"Elsie!" he said. "I'm so glad you came." Before I sat down, he planted a peck on my cheek.

I returned it, more out of surprise than anything. He smirked rather triumphantly, and I reddened.

"How was your concert?" I asked once we were installed, me with a cup of tea and a large slice of chocolate cake and Jules with a cup of black coffee, at the table.

"Oh, the Viers Trio. Yes, I saw them on Friday. Jazz fusion, trumpet-dominated. Really quite good."

He spoke as though hearing live music were no big deal and as though he barely recalled the show he'd seen less than forty-eight hours earlier. When we first met, I'd found this offhand assurance attractive. He seemed to have stepped out of a British novel, and I'd been astonished that someone with his looks, intellect, and pedigree wanted me, Elsie Farrell from Bleecker Street.

"I'm glad you enjoyed it," I said. "Lila and I went to a concert on Friday night. We saw Serval at the Free Trade Hall."

"Oh, yes, I recall you mentioned something of the sort on Friday."

"It was good. We were even invited to the afterparty afterward. At the Piccadilly Hotel." Although I spoke casually, I peered over my teacup to see what effect this news would have on him.

Jules smiled indulgently. "And the rest of the weekend?"

Either my reports about the afterparty were the deluded ramblings of a harmless lunatic or invitations to concert afterparties were as mundane as trips to the launderette.

"Quiet. Work. And my family called yesterday."

Once again, he smirked. I had confirmed his suspicions: I was a goody two-shoes with no social life and certainly no romantic prospects beyond him.

I sipped my tea. "How's the dissertation coming?" That was why he had invited me after all.

Jules was doing his degree over two years unlike most of us who had to complete ours in a twelve-month period. Now, in his second year, he was working on his dissertation.

"I'm making progress," Jules replied. "I'm now contrasting the American and British treatment of personal and political freedom in the modern novel. There's a passage about Hemingway's work, and I'm not sure I've got it right. I was hoping you'd take a look at it."

"I'm happy to read it."

"I'd wanted to bring it to the caf, but when you came in, I checked my bag, and it appears I've forgotten it. If you'd like to come back to my flat, you could take a look at it, and I could give you another cuppa."

I hesitated. "All right." I had agreed to help him with his dissertation after all.

Yet again, Jules smirked. I repressed the urge to slap him.

Near the university, Jules's flat was on the third floor of a Georgian house with city views. With its drinks table, deep leather sofa, tinted glass coffee table, color television, and modern art prints, the lounge looked like a magazine spread of the intelligent bachelor's pad.

Of course, Jules could afford it, I reflected as I stepped over the threshold. His father was a successful barrister, a Queen's Counsel, in London, his maternal grandfather was a baronet, a Sir Andrew something, and Jules himself had been educated at Harrow and Cambridge. It was why he could devote two years to part-time study without working.

Gingerly, I sat on the leather sofa. It had been two weeks since I'd last been in the flat. How many times Belle had been there during that fortnight? I wondered if I cared.

Jules stopped by the drinks table. "Care for a drink?"

"No, thanks. A cup of tea would be lovely, though."

"What's this? A new prohibition against drinking during the day? Do I detect the influence of Mrs. Barrymore?"

"Of course not. I just don't feel like a drink, that's all. Now, I'm happy to look at your dissertation."

"Here it is." Jules handed me a spiral-bound notebook. "I'm interested to see what you make of the bit about Hemingway. Now, I'll put the kettle on."

He uttered this somewhat ironically, so I couldn't help smiling.

I was dimly aware of kitchen sounds—Jules putting on the hob and getting out tea things—while I read his dissertation. That is, the several pages he had written.

Jules was a good writer, his prose as assured as the firm capitals he printed with his black felt-tipped pen. But what his draft had in style it lacked in substance. He made broad statements about the link between political and personal freedom in the modern novel, but he didn't consistently support his claims with evidence. And somehow, by the fourth page, personal freedom had somehow become synonymous with sexual freedom.

"Well, what's the verdict, then?" Jules entered the lounge, a steaming mug of tea in one hand and a glass of red wine in the other. Handing me my tea, he sat beside me on the sofa and leaned back with the air of one about to receive joyful tidings.

"Your style is excellent," I began haltingly. I'd always been reluctant to criticize others' work.

His smile broadened.

"And I think the comparison between Greene and Hemingway is promising."

His smile became a smirk.

"That said, I think you could strengthen the comparison by adding a couple specific examples from their novels."

The smirk froze.

"Also, while you define political freedom, you never describe personal freedom. And somehow personal freedom turns into sexual freedom here, where you discuss the love scene from *For Whom the Bell Tolls*."

"Is sex such a problem?" asked Jules, smiling.

I refused to rise to the bait.

"It's fine—you just need to strengthen the transition and the connection between personal freedom and sexual liberation, especially if you're equating them. And be sure to define personal freedom early on."

The smirk reappeared.

"But it's self-evident, isn't it?"

"What is?"

"That all freedoms are one," said Jules. "That's why I didn't define them in the introduction. And I've every intention of inserting examples in the final draft. Now, I'm just collecting my thoughts on paper."

Oh why didn't he ask Belle about it? Why bother me when he chose to argue with every suggestion I made?

"Well, you know what you're doing anyhow." I drained my tea and rose from the couch. There seemed no reason to linger if he was going to refute every suggestion I made.

"Do I?" he murmured.

Setting aside his wine, he pulled my arm and propelled me back down beside him. Then his hand was behind my neck, and his mouth was on mine.

I returned his kiss. Wasn't this what I'd wanted for the past week and a half?

We rose from the sofa, and Jules led me to the bedroom with its large bed and the walnut wardrobe with its cubist cabinets. He kissed me again and began unbuttoning my blouse.

I stood there and let him undo my buttons And somehow, I thought of Alec and the kiss outside the Piccadilly's bar. I remembered his rough northern voice and his dark eyes and the musky scent that lurked behind the leather.

"I can't do this," I said.

"What?" said Jules. He was unbuttoning the last button on my blouse, and his blue eyes were round and uncomprehending, like those of a surprised fish.

"I don't want to," I said. I buttoned my blouse and bent to grab my cardigan, which had fallen to the floor.

"When did you become such a prude?"

"Maybe I always was."

I grabbed my handbag from the lounge and my coat from the foyer, and I raced from the flat, down the stairs, and into the street.

I didn't realize I was still running until an old man shot me an alarmed glance from under his wool cap. Then I slowed down.

What had happened in the flat? Jules had once again made advances to me though whether or not he'd broken it off with Belle was unclear. Either way, it was insulting.

Going to bed with Jules would have seemed a travesty, not only because he'd taken up with Belle and not only because he seldom listened to a word I said.

In the last forty-eight hours, two men had attempted to go to bed with me, and I'd rebuffed both of them.

The only difference was I wanted to go to bed with one of them.

It was ludicrous, of course. Musicians were worse philanderers than Jules, and Alec would probably listen even less than Jules did. It was silly to dwell on his dark eyes or the feel of his lips on mine. He had given me a good anecdote to tell my sister and my friends back home, and that was all. I would never see him again, and that, as my mom would say, was a blessing.

Rain fell, and as the drops hit my face, I picked up speed again. It would be good to be home and warm. Perhaps Lila and I could have a cuppa, and I could tell her about my visit with Jules.

When I entered the house, Mrs. Barrymore bustled out of the front room, frowning. Her frown lifted a bit when she saw me.

"Oh, Miss Farrell, thank goodness you're here. A young man's rang for you."

Was Jules so full of himself that he couldn't take no for an answer even after I'd fled his flat?

"Thank you." I stepped forward. I would be firm and decisive with Jules, even more than I had been at the flat.

"His name is Alec or Alec," said Mrs. Barrymore. "Northern by the sound of it. Anyhow, this is the second time he's rung this afternoon."

Six

It couldn't be. What were the chances that someone like Alec would want to see me again? I'd rebuffed his advances twice. Perhaps it was someone pretending to be Alec although I couldn't imagine who would play such a prank.

I followed Mrs. Barrymore into the front room, where she handed the telephone to me almost ceremoniously. She folded her arms, regarding me grimly as I brought the receiver to my ear.

"Hello?" I said. My voice was small, young, and probably more American than ever.

"Hello, Elsie, this is Alec. Alec Wilder from Serval." I recognized the northern accent.

"Hi, Alec." My voice was still small.

Mrs. Barrymore pursed her lips. Rather than face her, I turned and stared at a faded Cornish beach scene. Still, I felt her eyes on me.

"How's your weekend been, then?" he asked.

"All right. Work, mostly, and tea with a friend." It was true, depending on how you defined friend.

"Well, that's more productive than mine. Friday night was rather a late one, so I was no good to anyone—least of all myself—on Saturday." He chuckled. "I've just been at home today, playing guitar."

"Nice." Now I was becoming monosyllabic. He would lose interest for sure.

"Listen, Elsie, I sense you can't really talk, but can I see you again?"

My throat was dry. "Yes, I suppose so." That was neither keen nor cool, but academic indifference.

If Alec thought my response funny, he gave no sign of it.

"I've got stuff going on most of this week—we're in the recording studio for a few days—but I could be in Manchester again on Thursday. Do you want to have dinner? "

"Sure." An Americanism. I supposed it was inevitable.

"Do you like Italian food?"

"I love it. It's what we eat where I'm from."

"There's a little place called Isola Bella on Booth Street; I always go there when I'm in Manchester. Would you like to eat there?"

"I'd love to."

"Good. I'll fetch you at seven. What's your address?"

I told him, and we hung up. When I replaced the receiver, Mrs. Barrymore was staring at me, arms still folded, lips still puckered in disapproval.

"Who was that?" she asked.

She was the one who handed me the phone and told me it was a man named Alec with a northern accent.

"Alec Wilder. I met him last week." There was no reason to reveal how we met or what he did for a living.

"And what did he want?" Mrs. Barrymore's green eyes narrowed behind her round glasses.

She'd overheard my half of the whole exchange, for God's sake. Surely, it wasn't that hard to deduce our plans.

"We're going to dinner on Thursday."

Mrs. Barrymore snorted. "What became of the other young man?"

If she thought I was capable of juggling two men, she gave me more credit than anyone else ever had. "We're no longer seeing each other."

"Hmph. Well, this one sounds polite anyway," she said grudgingly.

Mrs. Barrymore had always distrusted Jules, probably because of the condescending tone he'd employed with her. Come to think of it, her dislike was understandable.

"How was church?" I asked, more to change the subject than anything.

"All right," she replied. "And it would have been even better if Sarah Hughes didn't think she was Queen of the Sunday School." She sniffed with derision. The pretensions of Mrs. Hughes to Anglican sainthood were even more contemptible than her lodgers' real or suspected iniquities.

I willed myself to listen to her account of Mrs. Hughes's antics with the Sunday school. Then I walked upstairs, trying to make sense of the last two hours.

It was two o'clock on a Sunday afternoon, and I'd already rebuffed Jules and accepted a rock star's invitation to dinner.

I had so many questions. Why had Jules attempted to seduce me after taking up with Belle? What, for that matter, did Alec want? But the most pressing question was how Alec had gotten my number in the first place.

I knocked on Lila's door. "Fancy a walk?" I said when she opened it.

Two large books were open on her desk, but something in my tone must have made her say yes.

The January afternoon was cold and grey, and the damp breeze propelled us forward, so we walked with our hands in our coat pockets. We couldn't talk properly in the street, so I suggested ducking into the nearest pub. The King's Arms was only a little bigger than The White Mouse, and like The White Mouse, it catered more to locals than students.

After our walk, the King's Arms was cozy with its gaslights and the scent of warm ale. Pints in hand, we settled at a table in the far corner. Two stout men played darts, and three old men sat at the bar.

"So I almost went to bed with Jules today," I began.

Lila's delicately arched eyebrows shot up. Her eyes narrowed as I related what had transpired first at the café and then at the flat.

"Jules thinks I don't like him; I don't," she said quietly.

Then I described Alec's call with Mrs. Barrymore looking on. Lila seemed mildly amused, but not nearly as surprised as she had when I recounted my visit with Jules.

"So the question is," I said, "how did Alec get my number?"

"Oh, I gave it to Lucas," Lila replied. "He said his girlfriend was thinking of doing some Egyptian-inspired sculptures, so I told him to have her get in touch with me if she ever came to Manchester. I promised to show her round the museum."

"But did Lucas ask you for our number?"

"Yes."

"Alec put him up to it."

"He might have done. But I think Lucas's girlfriend is really keen on Egyptian art." A little smile flickered at the back of her grey eyes.

"I suppose I don't know what to think about Alec," I said. "I mean, a rock musician is bound to be everything Jules is, only more so—philandering, selfish, arrogant."

Lila lit a cigarette. "Probably. Still, I think you should just go with it. It's only having dinner after all."

But was that what Alec had in mind?

Seven

In the days that followed, it became increasingly easy to forget that I'd seen Serval live, much less that I had arranged a date with Alec Wilder, its lead guitarist. I had no real opportunity for private conversation with Lila, and naturally, we discussed neither the concert nor my assignation at breakfast or dinner. Besides, I was so consumed with lectures about seventeenth-century poetry, medieval drama, and eighteenth-century essays that my plans for Thursday became a hazy, but pleasant prospect, much like Christmas is to small children in July. And just as children, at a certain age, begin to wonder whether Santa Claus or Father Christmas really will visit, I thought it unlikely Alec would really appear on Mrs. Barrymore's doorstep at seven on Thursday evening.

In any case, I told myself rather sternly, Alec had something in common with Santa: if they did materialize, they were both likely to disappoint. After all, girls like me couldn't sustain the romantic interest of their fellow postgraduates, let alone a rock 'n' roller.

The date became real to me on Thursday at about one in the afternoon. I stopped at the English postgraduate office for a cup of tea. When I entered, a small group of people were conversing. No Jules, I noted, though Belle was there. I sat beside Larry on a settee and stirred my tea.

Belle sat opposite us on a stuffed green chair that looked faintly Victorian. "You all right, Elsie?" Without waiting for my reply, she continued, "Jules and I and some people are getting Chinese takeaways and going to the cinema tonight. It's a screening of avant-garde Japanese films. Want to join us?"

She smiled widely. She knew damn well I wouldn't.

"Thanks, but I have other plans," I replied in what I hoped was a cool tone.

Belle tossed her long red hair. "I suppose it is a little square for you."

I shook my head. "No, it sounds interesting. It's just that I'm going to dinner."

"The landlady and her church friends?"

Oh, wouldn't she ever quit?

"No," I said quietly. "Someone I met."

Belle's eyes became huge, and her full lips lost their perpetual smirk. Her bewilderment would have been hilarious if it hadn't been so insulting. Was it really so surprising that a man would ask me to have dinner?

"Come to think of it, Rogers and I would like a night in," said Larry, scratching his head as though it had just occurred to him. "We've both been so busy lately, it'll be good to just have dinner alone in the flat even if it's just egg and chips."

Stretched across a settee, Clara yawned. "I'll probably stay in and read tonight. If I get really ambitious and the cat permits me, I might nip to the off-license for a bottle of plonk and some chocolates."

Belle smirked, apparently amused by her coursemates and their lackluster social lives. I wondered about the "some people" who were accompanying her and Jules to the Chinese restaurant and the cinema. Were they as real as my dinner date?

Afterward, I found myself walking down Lime Grove to the library with Clara.

"Don't let Belle get to you," she said, taking a drag on her hand-rolled cigarette. "She's just jealous of your Marshall Scholarship. Has been ever since the course began."

"I hope I don't rub it in—"

"Rub it in? Of course, you don't rub it in. Belle just resents anyone who has anything she doesn't have. Like Jules."

"She's got him now."

"Are you all right, pet?"

"I wasn't. I am now." I was even surer now than I'd been when I'd spoke to my mom over the weekend.

"Glad to hear it. He's always put a bad taste in my mouth." She tossed her fag to the pavement and stubbed it rather vehemently with her toe. I repressed a smile, imagining her crushing all the world's prats beneath her brown loafer.

"And this new man?"

"Very new. I've only met him briefly. And it's just dinner." If we did end up going out.

"Yes, but it must be nice to be asked."

And though Clara smiled kindly and spoke cheerfully, I felt rather sad for her. After all, she didn't meet many people like her in Manchester or anywhere.

But I knew Clara wouldn't want me feeling sorry for her. "Well, we'll see," I said. "What did you think of Scott's lecture about morality plays in Cornwall?"

Later that afternoon, I reminded Mrs. Barrymore that I would not be home for dinner that evening. She was mashing potatoes in the kitchen, and when I spoke, her brow furrowed.

"So I'll make one less rib," she said.

"Thank you," I said. I was relieved she hadn't made more of a fuss. For all that Mrs. Barrymore grumbled about the expense of feeding four additional mouths, she often seemed resentful when we were absent for meals.

"Not that you seem very certain about it at all," she muttered, turning once more to her potatoes.

I opened my mouth, then shut it. Defending myself would only make matters worse.

But as I left the kitchen, Mrs. Barrymore could not resist one more parting salvo.

"If you do go out, just be sure you're back by ten," she said.

I grimaced as I shut the kitchen door behind me. Was it unlikely I'd forget her curfew after being reminded of it nearly every day for the past four months? And was it so preposterous that a man would like to take me to dinner? Jules, after all, had taken me out quite a few times.

There was nothing for it, but to get ready for my increasingly unlikely and no doubt imaginary date. In any case, if my mythical rock star did not appear by half-past seven, I would be exceptionally well-dressed for a stroll to the nearest chippie.

But just in case Alec Wilder really did materialize, I put on my black corduroy skirt, black turtleneck sweater, and high black boots. And this time, my curls behaved themselves: that is, they did not devolve into frizz. Mascara and coral lipstick completed my toilette.

I smiled as I surveyed my reflection in the full-length mirror. I lacked Belle's bold assurance and Lila's beauty, but I was pleased with myself. I looked, I hoped, sufficiently hip for a date with a rock musician, but in an understated sort of way, the sort that suggested I might be clever enough to be enrolled on a master's course.

To be sure, it was a lot to expect of a skirt, sweater, and boots. And as Belle would no doubt be only too happy to tell me, fashion had never been my thing.

Neither had romance. I'd had a boyfriend, briefly, in high school, a few dates in college, and then Jules. And look at how that had turned out.

I got romance horribly wrong. There was something about me that either put men off or attracted the wrong ones. I would probably end up putting Alec off, or he would be one of the wrong ones. Of course, I reflected, "and," not "or," was the appropriate conjunction. Then I laughed at myself. Only a certain type of graduate student would view her love life in grammatical terms. I was it.

From downstairs, I heard Mrs. Barrymore's doorbell ring. I glanced hurriedly at the clock. Ten till seven. Alec had not only appeared; he had done so ten minutes early. Not very rockstarish of him. If it was Alec, that is.

I peered out the window onto the street. A light blue car I didn't recognize was parked opposite the house.

Lila was on the landing when I stepped out of my room, a Cleopatra in jeans and a black cardigan.

"You look nice," she said with a smile. "Tell me how it goes."

I stepped downstairs briskly. I didn't want to keep Alec waiting, I didn't want to appear too eager, and I didn't want Mrs. Barrymore to get to the door before I did.

I failed on the third count. At least, I arrived at the bottom of the stairs to find Mrs. Barrymore poised by the front door, both hands on her hips.

"I'm sure I can open my own door," she said. "And should you be wearing such a short skirt?"

Eight

Fortunately, the question proved a rhetorical one, for after giving me a hard stare, Mrs. Barrymore opened the front door. From my vantage point, I couldn't see who was on the doorstep.

"Good evening," she declared.

"Good evening," said a northern voice. "I'm Alec Wilder."

I gulped. It was him after all. I didn't know whether to be relieved or alarmed.

"Ann Barrymore." Mrs. Barrymore inclined her head slightly.

"It's lovely to meet you. Is Elsie in?"

"Miss Farrell is at home," she said heavily.

"We've got plans for this evening."

She made no reply, but stared stonily out, her hand on the doorknob.

It was 1973, my date was standing on the front step, and my landlady showed every sign of trying to prevent us from going out.

"If you could let her let her know I'm here—"

I could contain myself no longer. "Hello, Alec," I said, stepping into the foyer.

"Hello, Elsie," he said. "You look lovely." His brown corduroy sport coat managed to look both casual and polished, and his dark eyes smiled into mine.

"Hmph. Well, you know curfew's at ten." Behind her glasses, Mrs. Barrymore glared at me, one hand still on the doorknob. I wondered whether she was trying to prevent me from leaving or staying.

"Thank you, Mrs. Barrymore, good evening," I said as I stepped out the door.

"Yes, good evening, Mrs. Barrymore, lovely to meet you," said Alec.

My landlady muttered something that might have conveyed reciprocation and shut the door rather vehemently.

Alec and I were alone in Mrs. Barrymore's front garden.

He smiled, his eyes alight with merriment.

"I'm sorry," I said. "That was unspeakably rude."

"On the contrary, I'm grateful she's entrusting me with you for three hours. Shall we go? My car's parked just over there." He gestured at the pale blue sedan across the street.

He held open the passenger door for me. That was gentlemanlike, I thought as I fastened my seatbelt. Mom and Nana would approve of that gesture at least.

Alec started the car. "It's a short drive to Isola Bella," he said. "That Italian restaurant I told you about. If you're still keen."

"Of course, I'm keen. It's what we eat where I'm from."

He glanced at me. "Jersey City?"

"Good memory."

"You're rather memorable, Elsie."

And how many girls had he said that to? I decided to steer the conversation into safer channels.

"How was your week?" I asked.

"All right. Busy. Lots of time in the recording studio." He spoke of it the way other men might refer to an office or factory.

"How did it go?"

"A bit boring to be honest. We were in the studio for twelve hours yesterday. Lots of takes on a few songs. A lot of effort for relatively little return."

"I never thought of recording studios as particularly dull."

"They can be. When the songs come together, it's magical. When they don't, it's just like any other job. And we spend about fourteen hours there some days."

We were entering the center. Under streetlights, groups and pairs of people hurried into pubs and restaurants, their lighted windows promising warmth and conviviality.

Alec maneuvered the car into a small side street. "How was your week, Elsie?"

"Full of libraries and lectures."

"It sounds idyllic."

His voice was serious. Surreptitiously, I stole a glance at his profile. There was no irony there either.

"It is, I suppose. I'm lucky to spend a year immersing myself in literature. I'm just surprised—"

"To hear me say that."

"Yes."

Alec reversed the car into a parking spot. Once he'd parked the car, he turned to me.

"I was seventeen when I left A-levels to pursue music. I was quite good at English and languages and history. I don't regret that decision at all, but it doesn't mean I don't think about what might have been."

I nodded. I could see that.

The restaurant was just across the street. The air was damp and cold, and I shivered as we crossed the street. Alec stuck his hands deep in his pockets.

Isola Bella was on the ground floor of a coral stone Victorian building. As Alec opened the door, the smell of garlic and oregano greeted us. Low hanging lamps and candlelight cast a soft glow over the interior.

A middle-aged waiter with olive skin met us. "Good evening, Mr. Wilder," he said in an Italian accent. "Two for dinner?"

He led us to a small alcove at the rear of the restaurant. The table had already been laid for two—perhaps Alec had reserved it—and two white candles in wine bottles gleamed atop it.

"Can I start you off with something to drink?" asked the waiter. "A bottle of the 65 Chianti perhaps? Or if the lady prefers white wine, the 68 Chenin blanc?"

"What will it be, Elsie?" asked Alec.

"Well, I generally prefer white, but with Italian food, red."

Alec smiled. "The Chianti then."

"Very good, Mr. Wilder."

We were alone. "This place is lovely," I said.

"Glad you like it. I always come here when I'm in Manchester."

Of course, he did. They knew him. I wondered how many other women he'd brought to Isola Bella.

The waiter returned with the wine and two glasses. He poured it rather ceremoniously, and then took our orders. I ordered a plate of spaghetti and meatballs, while Alec chose chicken parmesan.

I appreciated that Alec didn't tell me what to eat. Jules, while he had never actually forced anything down my throat, had always been after me to eat things I didn't fancy: seafood or escargot or caviar. Then again, I couldn't imagine Jules in an Italian restaurant. Dates in an Italian restaurant were a cliché, and Jules, as he always avowed, despised clichés.

"Oh, Elsie," he'd say, shaking his head in mock dismay. "Do you eat nothing but meat and potatoes and Italian food? You might almost be British, you know, with a palate like that. Thank God, you've branched out to curry."

Alec sipped his wine. "So you eat a lot of Italian food at home. Do you have Italian blood then?"

"No, my family's German and Irish on both sides. But a lot of Italians immigrated to New York and New Jersey, so Italian food has become the regional cuisine."

"Like curry in Britain."

"Pretty much."

"What else was it like at home?"

"What in particular?" I wasn't accustomed to men asking me about home. Certainly Jules never had.

"Your family, whether you have brothers or sisters, that kind of thing."

"My dad's an autobody repairman; my mom's a housewife. I have a sister, Maggie, who's three years older than I am. She lives just around the corner with her husband and their two-year-old son, Patrick. My nana, my maternal grandmother, lives with my parents. We have a tabby cat named Emily and a dog, a corgi mix called Nellie."

"You miss them?"

"I suppose I do. Not every minute of every day, but when something funny or annoying happens, I'm disappointed that I can't tell Maggie or my mom about it right away. We talk on the phone once a month, though. And naturally, I miss Emily and Nellie."

"You're a lucky girl, Elsie Farrell," he said quietly.

Our plates arrived. When the waiter left, I returned to the subject of our backgrounds.

"Where did you grow up?" I asked.

"North Yorkshire," replied Alec. "Reston, a little village not far from Northallerton."

"Now that sounds idyllic."

"For the most part, it was. Like your dad, mine worked on cars; he was a mechanic, and he owned a small repair shop. Like your mum, mine's a housewife. She does a lot of voluntary work in the village, teaching Sunday school and such."

"Do you have brothers and sisters?"

"One brother, three years older." He was concentrating very hard on his chicken parmesan.

Clearly, he didn't want to talk about it. I wracked my brains for a way to change the subject.

"Why is the band called Serval?"

Alec smiled almost shyly.

"When I was growing up, my family had a cat named Bob. He looked bit like a lynx because he had little tufts at the top of his ears. When the band started and we tossed around names, I suggested Lynx. But we wanted an animal most people hadn't heard of. I looked through a book about wildcats I'd had as a boy, and we settled on Serval. It also sounded like servile, so that gave it a bit of an edge."

"I can see that. Do you have a cat now?"

Alec shook his head. "I wish I did, but I'm away from home too much, and I can't ask the cleaner to look after anything for me. My mum's got two cats, though. She started a chapter of Cats Protection in her village."

"Do you get to see the cats?"

Alec shifted in his chair and jabbed at his chicken. "I've not been home in a while, so no."

Apparently, all roads led to home. I resolved not to bring it up again.

This time, Alec changed the subject. "So what were your lectures about this week?"

We ordered coffee and dessert, two cannoli. As we left the restaurant, we passed a couple at a small table. Alec exchanged nods with the man, who was strikingly handsome with chin-length dark hair, high cheekbones, and a beard.

"Who was that?" I asked as we stepped into the January night.

"George Best. Plays for Man United."

"You know him?" I didn't follow soccer, or football as the English called it, but I had heard of George Best.

"We've met at a couple parties."

The temperature had dropped, and I shivered.

"You all right, Elsie?" Alec put his arm around my shoulder and drew me close as we crossed the street. Once again, I smelled the muskiness I thought of as him.

"Thank you for dinner," I said when we were inside the car.

"The pleasure was all mine."

Then he kissed me as he had outside the Piccadily's bar, first on the mouth and then on the collarbone, his stubble tickling my neck.

His breath was on my ear. "What do you say to a nightcap at the hotel?" Then his lips were on my neck again.

He must have heard the slight intake of breath for he stopped kissing me and met my eyes.

"I can't," I said. "Mrs. Barrymore's curfew is at ten." Why did I always sound about fourteen when I talked to men?

"Well, we can't disappoint Mrs. Barrymore," he said lightly as he started the car. "So how has Manchester proven thus far?"

We talked about inconsequential subjects on the way home. I asked him about Lucas, and he inquired politely about Lila though he called her Lisa.

"It's Lila," I said in mock reproof.

"I'm sorry. She seems like a very nice girl; I just didn't pay much attention to her."

This was hard to believe given that most men, including his bandmate, gaped at Lila.

When we were parked outside Mrs. Barrymore's rowhouse, Alec smiled at me. "So I've gotten you home all in one piece, and it's just half-past nine. Surely, that will get me in Mrs. Barrymore's good graces."

"The road to her good opinion is very narrow. Two of the other lodgers have it, Lila doesn't, and I'm rapidly losing any ground I had."

"I hope I won't compromise that if I see you again. Are you about next weekend?"

"Yes." I hadn't expected him to suggest a second date. Perhaps he was just being polite. "The thing is, I'm supposed to spend most of Saturday at a symposium. One of my lecturers and a friend from my course are presenting papers about medieval literature."

Alec nodded as if it were the most normal thing in the world. "I'll come."

"To the symposium?"

"Why not? I've never been to one, and it sounds interesting."

He was being nice. He'd be bored stiff with a bunch of dusty academics. It was hard enough to attract scholars from other areas to symposia.

"If you're quite sure—"

"If you don't want me there, I understand." There was resignation in his voice and some embarrassment.

"No, I just thought you'd be bored." Perhaps this was his way of getting out of another date with me.

"With you there? Most assuredly not."

I wondered, once again, how many women he'd said that to. Then he pulled me close, and there was only the warmth of his mouth on mine.

Alec walked me to Mrs. Barrymore's front door.

"Good night, Elsie," he said. "I'll ring in a few days." A peck on the lips and then he was off in his blue car.

Perhaps the last couple hours hadn't really happened. I had walked to the chippie, and the date was a reverie born of fish and chips with a side of vinegar and delusion.

I rang the doorbell. Mrs. Barrymore opened the door, holding her pink dressing gown close as though she might be concealing a weapon beneath it. Behind her glasses, she stared coolly at me.

"Good evening, Mrs. Barrymore," I said brightly. "I do hope you've had a nice time."

"Some of us are abed at this hour, Miss Farrell," said Mrs. Barrymore coldly. "I will not inquire about your activities."

Meekly, I scurried into the house. This, at least, was reality.

Nine

"I'll say one thing for Mr. Wilder; he's got a very fine car," sniffed Mrs. Barrymore at breakfast the next morning.

Eyes bright, Ravi looked up from his eggs and toast. "What sort of car does he drive, Miss Farrell?"

I buttered my toast and considered. "Blue," I said finally. "A light blue sedan."

"A blue sedan!" said Ralph with more animation than usual. "It's a Mercedes S-class. I saw it from my window." His left eyebrow twitched.

I shrugged. "I've always been hopeless at cars." It was true. I took after my mom. To her, highways were filled with little red cars and big green ones and large blue trucks, not the Volkswagons and Cadillacs and Chevys that fired others' imaginations. Maggie always laughed at our lack of car knowledge.

Over her cup, Mrs. Barrymore's eyes narrowed. "What does Mr. Wilder do that he can afford a car like that?"

"He's a musician," I said. I hoped she wouldn't ask what sort.

She did. "What kind of music does he play?"

To Mrs. Barrymore, rock musicians were only one step above drug dealers and pimps—and not a very big step at that. I opened my mouth, but no words emerged.

"Mr. Wilder is a great musician," said Ravi. "In fact, he is one of the first violinists of the Royal Philharmonic Orchestra. How I long to hear Mr. Alec Wilder perform a solo during a Mozart sonata. I hope to have this experience when I am next in London."

I leaned back in my chair. Ravi was proving relentlessly inventive. He would make a good defense lawyer.

"He's in an orchestra? With that long hair?"

"Well, you know, Aunt Ann, they're all very artistic," said Ralph.

Mrs. Barrymore seemed to consider this. Then she nodded.

"Yes," she said finally. "I suppose they are."

"Thank you," I mouthed to Ravi when she withdrew to the kitchen.

"Don't mention it, Miss Farrell," he replied cheerfully. "If I can have the pleasure of shaking hands with the great violinist, it will be ample reward."

"Believe me," I said fervently, "if I can arrange it, I will."

I received three calls on Saturday afternoon.

The first was from my mom. "How are you, sweetie?" she asked.

There was an extra tenderness in her voice. What had brought this on? Was she merely sentimental? Then I realized she was still concerned about me: after all, only a week ago, I had told her about splitting up with Jules. The poor woman had spent a week imagining me crying in my rented room or dodging Jules at the library. No wonder she had splurged on a transatlantic call.

"So have you been having fun with your friends?" she asked with forced brightness.

"Yes." I decided to tell her the whole story. If I didn't mention Jules, she'd assume I was putting on a brave face.

"Last Sunday, I had tea with Jules," I began.

"Oh." Mom was incapable of hiding her feelings.

"It's fine, Mom. I agreed to see him because he said he wanted my help with an essay. He didn't, really. I won't be seeing him again."

"Oh, good." Her relief, like her dismay, was audible.

"But I had a date on Thursday night."

"Oh?"

I couldn't help but smile at her excitement. "Yes. With a man named Alec. He took me to an Italian restaurant in the center. Downtown."

She wanted to know all about it, what I wore, what the restaurant was like, what we ate and drank. She laughed when she heard what Mrs. Barrymore had said about my skirt. Because my landlady was at the shop, I could speak frankly.

"Will you be seeing Alec again?" she asked.

"I think so. He said he'd be back in Manchester next weekend. Larry—you know, that nice man from my course—is going to be speaking at a symposium about medieval literature. I'm going, and Alec said he'd go with me."

"Oh, what a nice man! Oh, honey, I'm so happy for you. And your father and Nana will be happy, too. Nana has been saying novenas for you, and I've been praying, too."

"It's just a second date." But I was touched to think of them praying that I would find a husband or, at the very least, a reliable boyfriend.

"But it's nice to go out with a nice man. Oh, I forgot to ask you, what does Alec do for a living?"

"Alec. He plays in a band. The one Lila and I went to see last week."

I braced myself. Mom, like Mrs. Barrymore, had very definite opinions about what she called musician types.

"Oh!"

But Mom was no Mrs. Barrymore. She only missed a beat. "He sounds like a nice man. I can't wait to tell your father and Nana. They'll be so happy!"

A few minutes after we hung up, Alec called.

"Hello, Elsie," he said. "I'm pleasantly surprised to get you on the line. I was anticipating the disapproving tones of your august landlady."

"You just might have insinuated your way into her good graces. All inadvertently, of course."

Alec laughed heartily when I recounted what had transpired during Friday's breakfast.

"So it's because of Ravi I'm allowed to take you out again. I owe him a pint. In fact, your fellow boarders should come out for a pint after the symposium. The other bloke and Linda, too."

"Lila," I said sternly.

"I'll get it right one of these days."

We chatted for a bit and then he rang off. "I certainly don't want to be accused of engaging Mrs. Barrymore's line for too long. Especially if she expects me to play the violin for her."

After I hung up the phone, I sat for a few minutes on Mrs. Barrymore's green settee. I was dimly aware that there was a dopey grin on my face, and I didn't care. I was loved by two people who prayed I would find a husband, and I'd met a man who was happy to accompany me to what would no doubt be a dull affair to anyone uninterested in medieval literature. A man who played guitar in a rock band, drove a light blue car that was, apparently, a Mercedes, and had velvety dark eyes.

The phone rang, startling me from my reverie. "Hello?" I answered cheerfully. Somehow, I expected to hear Alec's voice again.

But the voice that answered mine was female, querulous, and high-pitched. "Is Elsie Farrell in?"

"She most certainly is, Mrs. Parrolli." My sister Maggie had always enjoyed disguising her voice, and the whiny falsetto was her specialty.

"Mom said you met someone."

Even on a transatlantic call, Maggie was never one to bother with the preliminaries, not when she had a mission. Mom must have gotten on the phone to her as soon as we'd hung up.

"Well, it's just one date," I replied. "And we have plans for next weekend." Once again, I summarized our date at Isola Bella and next week's symposium.

"Wow, it sounds like he really likes you!" said Maggie. And even though she'd been married for four years and been a mother for two, she sounded as ebullient as she had when we'd shared a room as teenagers and exchanged confidences into the night.

Next came the inevitable. "How did you meet?"

I told the truth, minus the invitations to his hotel room. Close as we were, I knew the unvarnished truth would horrify her.

It was still too much.

"Elsie, how could you?" Maggie exclaimed.

There was no way to answer this, so I said nothing.

"Does Mom know?" she asked in a hushed voice.

"That he plays in a band. Yes." I flattered myself that I kept the smile from my voice. For that Maggie had railed against our parents' overprotectiveness when we were teenagers, she was, in some ways, less liberal than our Catholic mother.

"She can't really know. Or if she does, she's just being nice about it. Elsie, I love music as much as anyone, but I would never date a musician. All the groupies and the drugs—"

"Margaret. I am twenty-three. I am a graduate student. Postgraduate as they say here. I do not take drugs. I have not tried marijuana. I don't even smoke, for Chrissake. I am hardly going to be enticed into drug addiction."

"You laugh, but of course, I'm worried. If you're in love with this man, you'll be swept up into it all—"

Her voice broke. "It's just that you're my baby sister, and I don't want you to be hurt. Or used!"

This time, I spoke gently. "Maggie, I'm here to earn a degree, remember? And in less than a year, I'll go back to the States and teach and maybe apply to PhD programs. And we've only had one date. Next weekend, we're supposed to hear one of my friends and some dusty academic types read papers about medieval literature. I'm sure he can find something better to do between now and then."

Even Maggie laughed at that. And for a few minutes, I got her to chat about her life. Patrick could express himself in sentences now; that is, he could ask for his favorite foods, bananas and toast. And he'd definitely asked when Aunt Elsie would come again.

We hung up on good terms. And yet, as I sat back on Mrs. Barrymore's green stiff settee, my spirits sank.

I didn't fear that I'd become a groupie or a drug addict. But perhaps Maggie had a point. By pinning my hopes on someone like Alec, I was setting myself up for hurt. Even if he wanted to buy drinks for my fellow lodgers. Even if he was willing to listen to dull papers to spend a Saturday with me.

I'd spoken flippantly, but perhaps the best thing that could happen was for Alec to go off the symposium between now and Saturday. He had agreed to go on a whim; perhaps he would meet someone more alluring, and an equal and opposite impulse would overtake him in the next seven days.

Ten

The symposium, much like the dinner at Isola Bella, seemed unreal to me until it happened.

The day before, a few of us chatted about it in the postgraduate office. "Of course, I'm going," Clara declared. "I couldn't not support you and Scott. Besides, some of the papers sound interesting."

"And I'm coming as well," I said "Looking forward to it."

"Thanks," said Larry. His hand shook as he took a drag on his cigarette. If he was this nervous the day before the presentation, what would he be like at the symposium itself?

"Sally coming?" asked Clara.

Larry shook his head. "She tried, but no one could cover for her."

"We should all go to the pub afterward," I said. "For a celebratory drink. Sally can join us when she gets off work, and I'll invite my fellow lodgers and perhaps another friend, too."

I hadn't wanted to mention Alec before the event in case he evaporated. But I wanted to give Larry something to look forward to after his presentation.

Larry smiled shyly. "Thank you," he replied in his deep voice.

I felt eyes on me. I turned to see Belle regarding us intently from the settee where she perused, or pretended to peruse, a book. She smiled rather superciliously at me. I did not return her smile.

"You'll be brilliant, Larry," she called. "Don't let them undermine your confidence."

Her back to Belle, Clara rolled her eyes.

The door opened, and Jules strolled in, carrying a mustard-colored sport coat over his shoulder. "What's this?" he asked.

"Larry's presenting at the medieval symposium tomorrow, and I was just saying how brilliant he'll be," simpered Belle.

"Oh, right," said Jules absently. "Though I have no time for medieval literature, of course. The dry remains of a desiccated culture."

It sounded like something a politician would utter, the sort who would vacillate between literary allusion and rage. The right-wing Tory Enoch Powell, perhaps, if Jules didn't like to think of himself as fashionably left.

"All the same, we should support each other," said Belle with a titter.

"For all that show, I don't think she'll come," I remarked later as Clara and I crossed the quad later that afternoon.

"I expect she will," said Clara. "She can't bear to be left out of anything, even conversations and events she doesn't care about. Did you see her staring at us in the office? Oh, well. If she does attend, she'll make a fuss of poor old Larry. And he'll know it's rubbish, but he'll lap it up anyway.

"And well done for suggesting a drink afterward," she continued. "That perked Larry up a bit. So your fellow lodgers will join us. Will they come to the symposium, too?"

"Probably not. Lila's the only one who'd be interested, and she's pretty consumed with her research these days."

"You mentioned another friend. . ."

It would be hard to put one over on Clara.

"Alec," I said. "The man I had dinner with last week."

"He's coming to the symposium?"

"Yes."

"Is he a medievalist?"

"No."

"A scholar?"

"No. He is a reader, though." That much was true.

"Still, he must be very keen on you."

I smiled wryly. "We'll see." To most of the world, a medieval literature symposium was worse than death. Would someone like Alec endure it for someone like me?

But at nine the next morning, Alec presented himself at Mrs. Barrymore's front door. Once again, she insisted on opening the door. On this occasion, however, she beamed at Alec—as much as she was capable of beaming.

"Good morning, Mr. Wilder," she said. "You may come in. Does the orchestra have the day off?"

"Well, you know, you get away when you can," Alec replied as he stepped into the foyer. He wore a tweed jacket, so he could pass for an orchestral musician on his day off. His eyes met mine, and I hid a smile.

"I wonder how long we can keep up that ruse," I said once we were in his car.

"As long as we have to." His dark eyes surveyed me. "You look very kissable, Elsie. If it weren't broad daylight and you weren't a respectable postgraduate, I would kiss you now."

"Try anyway."

He kissed me on the mouth and placed a hand on my knee. For a moment, there was nothing in the world but his embrace.

We pulled away at the same moment.

"We'd better stop now while we still can." But his hand rested on my knee as he started the car, and it remained there for the duration of the drive.

When Alec and I entered the lecture hall with its oak paneling, about three-quarters of the seats were full. My eyes scanned the room.

"There's Larry," I said. "And that's Clara next to him." They were seated in the back row, which was exactly where Larry would sit even though he was one of the speakers.

Clara waved and motioned to two vacant seats beside them. Larry seemed distracted though he greeted us pleasantly enough. But when he heard Alec's name, he sat up a little straighter.

"Thanks for coming," he said, shaking Alec's hand.

"No, thanks for presenting, it all sounds very interesting."

Once again, I scanned the lecture hall. No Jules and no Belle. Perhaps Clara had got it wrong.

The symposium started. First, an old man with silky white hair and a fluty voice, a retired lecturer, spoke about the history of medieval scholarship at Manchester, a tradition of excellence that, he said, continued today. Then, he introduced the first speaker, a third-year undergraduate exploring irony in Arthurian romances.

At first, the student's voice shook, but it became steadier as he progressed through his paper. With his round face and glasses, he looked endearingly youthful though he was probably only a year or two younger than I. His argument was interesting, and I resolved to compliment him privately on his scholarship.

The lecture hall's oak door creaked open. Unconsciously, I glanced in the sound's direction. Jules and Belle stood in the entranceway. I caught Belle's eye, and she flashed a smile in my direction. Then her eyes bulged, and her smile evaporated. She nudged Jules, and his eyes got rounder when he looked at me. With those staring eyes, he rather resembled a fish. How had I ever fancied him?

They found seats on the other side of the hall, about a third of the way from the front. The seats were in the middle of the row, so they had to step over other people's feet to reach them. Typical of Jules and Belle to interrupt someone's presentation instead of waiting at the back until it was finished. It was funny, in a way, although it wasn't very fair to the boy at the podium.

Their reaction to me, or rather to Alec, had been amusing, too. But wasn't it, on some level, insulting? Was it really so astonishing I'd met a man?

I returned to my attention to Sir Perceval and irony.

There were questions then, most of them, thank God, friendly and encouraging. Then another third-year, a young woman, read a paper about female mystics. And then it was Larry's turn.

"Good luck," I whispered as he rose from his seat.

Larry stood at the podium, his tweed jacket too large for his thin frame. His arms trembled as he set his papers on the podium; they continued to shake as he cleared his throat.

"I wish I could staple his arms to his sides," Clara whispered. "He'd be fine then."

But his voice was deep and clear. And there was nothing wrong with his scholarship. He'd discovered a connection between nativity plays in Manchester and Ireland; elements common to both also appeared in a cycle in Liverpool.

Despite his apprehension, Larry acquitted himself well during the question and answer period. Even a grizzled lecturer from Durham couldn't stump him. Then there was a break, and the four of us moved into the office for a cup of tea.

"Well done," said Alec, gripping Larry's hand. "I don't know much about miracle plays, but I can see you do."

"Thanks." Larry smiled rather self-consciously.

"So you're saying this play, or parts of it anyway, came from Ireland? A sort of medieval cultural export?"

"Yes. Although we can't prove anything in the literary world. We can only suggest things and then support them as well as we can."

"So we can say nearly anything we like," said Clara. "But most of us don't say them as well as Larry."

The office door swung open, and Jules and Belle entered. Belle, sporting a purple dress and high heels, rushed to Larry's side and planted a kiss on his cheek.

"Well done, Larry!" she exclaimed. "You were marvelous."

Over her mug, Clara caught my eye as if to say, "I told you so."

Larry blinked. "Thanks!" he said vaguely.

"Clara, Elsie, it's so lovely to see you," Belle gushed. "Elsie, introduce us to your friend."

Why she used the first-person plural eluded me since Jules was on the other side of the room. But sensing he was included in the us, he joined the little group around the tea things.

"Alec, Belle and Jules, Belle and Jules, Alec," I said as gracefully as I could.

"Lovely to meet you," said Alec. He turned back to Larry. "You must have to know a lot to study this sort of thing, then. Latin, I'm guessing, and Old English."

Larry nodded. "I had Latin at school, but I've had to wrestle with the Anglo-Saxons a good bit. Fortunately, the plays themselves are in Middle English, which is easier to understand."

"You're lucky you had Latin at school," I said. "I always wanted to study it for its own sake, and I've had to start from scratch since I've come to Manchester."

"I had Latin at school, of course," said Jules. "But it all seems rather superfluous in 1973." He dismissed Caesar and Cicero with a wave of his hand. "And, of course, it has no relevance to my scholarship."

Belle tossed her hair. "Oh, I agree. And though Larry's writing is brilliant, I have little taste for classroom stuff."

"But it's harder, isn't it?" Alec murmured.

Jules emitted a sound that might have passed for a snicker. "What's that?'"

"Well, if you need to study Old English or Latin like Larry and Elsie do, doesn't that add another layer of difficulty to the course? When you come to it, they're learning a language in addition to doing research and going to lectures."

Belle tittered. "I wouldn't call Latin a language exactly."

"Then what would you call it?" asked Alec amiably.

Belle simpered, Jules smirked, and neither of them deigned to reply.

The break was over, so we headed back to the lecture hall. Larry and Alec walked in front of Clara and me. Alec asked Larry another question about his research.

"I don't say this often," whispered Clara, "but I like your bloke."

Was Alec my bloke? Probably not, but I wasn't about to argue with Clara. He'd reduced Jules and Belle to silence, and I was proud of him. I held my head a little higher than usual as I entered the lecture hall.

Eleven

There were a few more papers followed by a lunch break and then a few more papers.

"How about that drink, then?" asked Alec as the lecture hall emptied.

"I'll just ring Sally's ward to see if she wants to come round after her shift is done," replied Larry.

"Then let's choose a pub near the Royal Infirmary."

"The Dancing Bear will do," said Larry. "It attracts an older crowd, mostly working men, and the grub is pretty good. If you like savory pies and such."

"I do. Elsie? Clara?"

We nodded our assent, and then the four of us climbed into Alec's car. As we drove away, we passed Jules and Belle on the pavement. Their eyes and mouths were wide, and I couldn't resist giving them a slight wave as the Mercedes sped away.

With its gaslights, the Dancing Bear proved as cozy and unpretentious as Larry had described. A few older men chatted at small tables; two played darts. Larry and I used the phone box outside to make our calls. When I called Mrs. Barrymore's house, Lila answered. She promised to join us and suspected Ravi and Ralph would be up for the outing.

Back in the pub, Alec, Clara, and Larry stood near the bar.

"Thank you all for coming today," Larry said in his quiet way. "It means a lot. I'd like to buy the first round."

Alec opened his mouth and reached into his pocket. Then he seemed to change his mind.

"It was a pleasure," he said easily.

Once we had our drinks, we settled around a large round table, the only one that seemed likely to accommodate our party as it expanded.

"So what do you do, Alec?" asked Clara.

"I play guitar."

"That's why I know your name!" said Larry. "I have Serval's last album. "Trunks" is brilliant. All the tracks are good, though."

It turned out Larry played when he had time. Soon, he and Alec were discussing the relative merits of various brands of guitar.

"That explains the Mercedes, then," Clara murmured to me.

I laughed. "You know, I didn't even realize it was a Mercedes until Ralph told me. I thought it was just a blue sedan."

"You sound like my mum! But anyway, rock star or not, Alec seems like a nice bloke. And I became a fan the moment he reduced Jules and Belle to silence." Extracting tobacco and rolling papers from her bag, she began rolling a cigarette.

"I must admit, I enjoyed that."

"Who wouldn't? All those snide comments about classroom stuff were bad enough, but to say Latin isn't a language takes the biscuit." She laughed heartily. "What a couple of twits."

Just as we finished our drinks, the rest of our party arrived. Ravi, Ralph, and Lila came in together, and then Larry's wife, Sally, entered. Plump with brown eyes and curly dark hair, she was accompanied by a tall, thin girl. She introduced her companion as Angie, another nurse on her ward. There were introductions and handshakes all around.

"I'm hungry and thirsty," said Alec. "I'll get the next round— and food, if anyone's hungry."

And just like that, Alec bought pints, pies, and mash for nine people. I admired the way he treated the entire party without hurting anyone's pride or coming off as the great man. I was proud of him though I told myself I hadn't any right to be, not really. He probably found himself in situations like this all the time. His generosity had nothing to do with any particular interest in me.

After we'd given our orders at the bar, we arranged ourselves around the table. Sally and Lila had met before, and since Sally was artistic— she was a potter as well as a nurse—they found plenty to discuss. Ralph and Larry chatted comfortably about football, and Clara took a seat next to Angie. Alec sat between Ravi and me.

"Apparently, I owe you another drink, Ravi," said Alec. "It's due to your quick thinking that I'm allowed to take Miss Farrell out again. Although I'm not looking forward to regaling Mrs. Barrymore with a violin sonata."

Ravi grinned. "If I were a professional violinist, I would not bring my violin to Manchester. It would be too vulnerable, too valuable. I would be very sorry to disappoint Mrs. Barrymore, but I could not take the risk."

"Once again, you're two steps ahead of me. You've earned yet another pint."

Alec's arm was around my shoulder, and we talked with Ravi about Alec's music and Ralph's legal aspirations. He had hoped to practice law in New Delhi after completing his degree and pupilage, but now he was not so sure.

"I like it here in England," he said. "The food, the people, and, of course, the music. But we shall see. My family in is India, of course, and so is my fiancée."

"I didn't know you were engaged!" It occurred to me that I knew relatively little of my fellow lodgers apart from Lila.

Ravi smiled. "I do not speak of Rhada often though she is very bright and beautiful. Like you, she is studying for a degree in English literature, a bachelor of arts, not a master of arts at this time. We frequently exchange letters, however, and she is always eager to hear of my doings in England."

Our food arrived then, and since I was hungry, I tucked into my meat pie. It was served on a pile of mash and topped with gravy that nearly made me salivate. For a few minutes, the beef and carrots and gravy-soaked pastry absorbed me completely.

"Ravi is full of surprises," I said to Alec after a few bites. "I had no idea he was engaged."

"Your mates are a nice lot," said Alec. "I've enjoyed spending the day with them."

"Even if it meant a medieval studies symposium?"

"I enjoyed that, too, I promise you. It was pleasant to listen to people who know what they're talking about."

I couldn't resist. "Even Jules and Belle?"

"Who?"

"The people who spoke to us in the postgraduate office."

"Oh, yes, classroom stuff and Latin isn't a language." He chuckled. "What did you think of them?"

He shrugged and sipped his ale. "I didn't really. The guy seemed a bit of a prat, and you meet a lot of girls like that in my business."

I hid my smile in a mouthful of mash.

"So, when do I get to hear you present your research, Elsie?" asked Alec.

"Maybe this summer. My tutor mentioned conferences in Bristol and York. After I finish my dissertation."

"Royalist poets during the Protectorate?"

"I can't believe you remember that!" We'd discussed my research the night we met, but I'd assumed my words went in one ear and out the other.

"I guess I'm astonished an American knows so much about our history."

"We're not all gangsters and cowboys, you know."

"Just most of you."

I made as if to cuff his ears, he ducked, and we both laughed.

Across from us, Clara and Angie were chatting. Clara's eyes were narrowed in amusement, and while Angie had initially impressed me as plain, animation had softened her angular features, and her cheeks glowed. When she took out a cigarette, Clara lit it for her.

Perhaps Clara had finally found someone like her. I hoped so. Until quite recently, I realized, my wishes would not have been as generous. I hadn't known any women like her— not that I knew of, anyway— and I certainly wouldn't have dreamed of being mates with one. But Clara had become a good friend, and I knew she was lonely in her bedsitter. Besides, I wanted everyone to be as happy as I was with Alec's arm draped lazily around my shoulder.

"Excuse me, Elsie," said Ravi suddenly. "Since this is the night of confidences, I wonder if I might ask you a question?"

"Of course." I hoped he wasn't going to ask any awkward questions about Alec and me.

Ravi leaned over Alec, who, in turn, sat back in his chair.

"Is Lila seeing anyone?" he asked.

Was that all? "Yes. Why do you ask?"

"It is because of Ralph," he replied simply. "He has been pining for her ever since you and Lila moved into the house in the autumn."

"She lives with a bloke named Harry when she's not at uni," I replied. "He's an engineer. They have a flat near Bristol."

Ravi nodded. "I thought so." He swallowed the last bite of his pie.

Alec laughed. "You deduced his name, occupation, and address?"

"Not precisely. But every few weekends, Miss Hedges, that is, Lila, takes the train. It is always to see her aunt near Bristol. Either Lila is an unusually devoted niece, or she has a boyfriend. I have tried on many occasions to explain this to Ralph, but he will not listen."

"Why did he never ask Lila to go for a drink or lunch?" I asked.

"He is too shy."

"Oh." I looked at Ralph. He and Larry were chatting with Lila and Sally, and now, away from Mrs. Barrymore's scrutiny, I saw the worshipful glances he cast in Lila's direction. He was a nice sort, and I hated to think of him being disappointed.

"Poor Ralph," I said faintly.

"Oh, he will be all right." Ravi sipped his ale calmly.

"How do you know?" I demanded.

"Because she is not the only object of his interest," replied Ravi. "He is also keen on a Miss Adams, a typist at the barrister's chambers where he is clerk. I believe he would have asked Miss Adams for a date if it had not been for Lila."

"Well, I hope she doesn't mind being his second choice." I had been with Jules, and I knew the feeling.

"She will not know it, and he will soon come to think she was his first," said Ravi. "Miss Adams is just the sort of woman to make Ralph happy. She listens cheerfully when he talks about the test match or the car he hopes to buy one day. She is as beautiful as Miss Hedges, but in a different way: she has fair hair and blue eyes. And Miss Adams will satisfy even so exacting an aunt as our good landlady: she attends church and teaches in the Sunday school. In fact, I suspect Mrs. Barrymore will forgive her for being Methodist and not C of E."

"Yes, I expect she will." Miss Adams sounded like the sort of girl who would meet with even Mrs. Barrymore's approbation. And Ravi was right: she seemed far better suited to Ralph than Lila with her kohl-rimmed eyes and archaeological ambitions and decisive utterances.

But there was one question he hadn't answered.

"Ravi," I said. "Where did you tell Mrs. Barrymore you were going? Does she expect us to be back by ten?"

Ravi grinned. "Oh, that was easy. I told her Mr. Wilder and some of his friends were giving an impromptu concert. Chamber music. There would be a supper afterward, and it might go past ten. Mrs. Barrymore was very understanding."

Alec's shoulders shook. "Mate, if I ever need someone to sort out my life, I'll come to you."

Once again, Ravi smiled. "I will rely on it."

Twelve

After the next round, people began to talk of going home. Alec offered to ferry them in his car.

"We'll walk home," said Larry after a quick glance at Sally. "Night air will do us good, and besides, we're not far from the flat."

Clara and Angie were equally determined to walk, so that left my fellow lodgers and me to climb into Alec's Mercedes.

There was wonder in Ralph's eyes as he climbed into the backseat. Hiding a smile, I hoped he would one day be able to afford a car like this if it meant that much to him. Perhaps the excellent Miss Adams would sit beside him and they would be happy as I felt with Alec's arm around me.

When we parked opposite Mrs. Barrymore's house, my housemates had the tact to thank him for the lift and leave us alone in the car.

"Thank you for the lift and the drinks," I said. My voice was ridiculously small and young.

"And thank you for today," said Alec. Then he kissed me gently on the mouth.

"When can I see you again, Elsie?" he asked.

"I don't know," I replied. Somehow, it hadn't occurred to me that he would want to make plans to see me again after the symposium. "When were you thinking?"

"I could stay at the Midland another night," he said. "I don't really have to be back at the studio until Monday afternoon. Stretch a point and say Tuesday. Would you like to have dinner tomorrow?"

"Yes."

"Anything I should know about your likes and dislikes?"

"I love Italian food. I like English food and curries. I hate seafood."

Alec laughed. "Lobster's always stuck in my throat."

"It's cruel, isn't it, cooking something alive like that?"

"Barbaric. I can never enjoy it. Shall I pick you up at seven?"

He kissed me gently again, and I bid him good night as I stepped out of the car.

Cold air struck my cheek as I walked to Mrs. Barrymore's front door. That last bit didn't seem real. I'd just spent an entire day in Alec's company, and we were having dinner the next night. Girls like me didn't retain guys' interest for very long.

The next morning, Lila and I dissected the symposium and its aftermath over a cup of tea while Mrs. Barrymore was at church. She laughed when I recounted the exchange with Jules and Belle in the postgrad office.

"Latin not a language!" she scoffed. "Even Belle knows better than that. She was probably just showing off in front of Jules and Alec. And I would have loved to have seen Alec reduce them to silence. If I'd known that last night, I would have bought him a drink."

"What did you think of him?" I asked. She'd met him before, of course, but she'd barely spoken to him at The White Mouse and the after-party at the Piccadilly.

"He seems nice. Down-to-earth. I liked how he bought us all pints and pies without showing off."

From Lila, this was high praise.

"We're having dinner tonight."

Lila nodded. "Excellent."

I hesitated. "It just feels a bit unreal, that's all. Because of the way it started. Meeting in The White Mouse."

"I can see that. But people have to meet somewhere, don't they? Harry and I met at a club."

"Yes, but Harry didn't try to pull you."

"Alec's been nice since then. Maybe it started that way, and then he discovered he really liked you. I think you should just go with it."

Not for the first time, I wondered if I was congenitally incapable of going with it—if it meant romance or the possibility thereof.

In any case, that evening, I donned my favorite dress, a black wool turtleneck dress that ended just above the knee, and my high boots.

At five of seven, Mrs. Barrymore's doorbell rang. Mrs. Barrymore smoothed her hair and went to answer it while I waited in the front room.

"Good evening, Mr. Wilder," she said. "Please come in." Her voice was much pleasanter now that she believed he was with the Royal Philharmonic.

His boots clicked in the foyer. "Thank you, Mrs. Barrymore. These are for you."

"Why, Mr. Wilder, they're lovely. Thank you so much for thinking of me. How did you know I love yellow flowers?"

"Lucky guess."

My curiosity piqued, I stepped into the foyer. Mrs. Barrymore clutched a bunch of yellow carnations. Behind her glasses, her green eyes gazed fondly at them.

Alec wore a blue velvet jacket and heeled boots. His dark eyes smiled into mine.

"Hello, Elsie," he said.

He handed me a bouquet of pink roses. I counted ten, no a dozen, small, perfect blossoms.

"For me?" I said. No one had ever given me flowers before except for my uncle at my high school graduation.

The corners of his eyes crinkled. "Yes, you."

"Now, you be civil and thank Mr. Wilder," said Mrs. Barrymore. "It's kind of him to think of us. I'll put both of these in water to keep them fresh."

"I'm afraid I didn't thank you properly for the roses," I said as we drove away in the Mercedes. "But they're lovely."

"My pleasure." Alec lifted my hand to his lips, holding it there for a few seconds before releasing it. "You look beautiful, Elsie."

There was a little flutter of anticipation in my belly.

"I thought a bit about dinner tonight," he said, "and I narrowed it down to two places. There's a decent French restaurant, The French, at the Midland where I'm staying. Or we could try Isola Bella again. Your choice."

"They both sound good. And I've never had proper French food before. But I have to say Isola Bella."

"I can't say I'm disappointed."

Once again, the aroma of garlic and olive oil greeted us, and the waiter led us to the table for two at the restaurant's rear. This time, Alec ordered a cabernet sauvignon.

"It was lovely to meet your mates, Elsie," said Alec. "But I'm glad I can be alone with you tonight."

"I'm glad to be here."

"So will you be teaching when it's all said and done? The MA, I mean?"

I nodded. "I expect so."

The waiter returned to take our orders. When he left, Alec resumed the conversation.

"You expect to teach. Do you want to?"

"You're very perceptive, you know. Most of us expect to teach. I could get hired at a university back in the States. I might apply to American PhD programs when the course is over. It's fine; I just don't feel particularly excited about it."

My frankness surprised me. I hadn't articulated my ambivalence about teaching to anyone before, not even my family.

"What do you want to do?" There was no judgement in his tone, just curiosity.

"It's funny, but I don't really think of it. I don't let myself, really. Write, I suppose."

"What sort of things do you write?"

"Poetry, mainly. Badly. But I wouldn't mind doing some freelance writing for magazines and such."

"Could you keep writing while you teach?"

"Of course." I paused. "Like you with your side project."

"Touché. I'm impressed you remember it. Yes, it's harder to make time for that endeavor than you'd think although most people assume professional musicians don't do much of anything."

He hesitated. "Can I read it sometime? Your poetry?"

"Since you asked nicely. Really, it's not fit for anyone's consumption. But I'll show you the best bits."

Other than my family, few people had evinced interest in my verse. Perhaps this was his way of seducing me.

He asked about my family, and I soon found myself regaling him with anecdotes about our life in Jersey City. There was the time I'd embarrassed Maggie at the Italian deli, and there were Nana's astonished comments on every facet of modern life. And there were the summer nights when we slept over our grandparents' apartment when Poppa was still alive. We'd stay up late on the roof. From there, we could look across the Hudson and see the lights of Manhattan. Beneath us, the street teemed with people coming and going. Others, like us, sat on their roofs and balconies and front steps to escape the heat.

He laughed at all the right places. "People talk as though city childhoods are rough by definition, but you don't sound deprived, Elsie."

"I most definitely was not. My dad made enough money so that we could afford our own home. My parents both grew up poor, but my grandparents' apartments—flats—were warm places. You know, when I was growing up, I didn't even know they were poor. Both sets of grandparents were always taking Maggie and me to the cinema and buying us ice cream."

"But you got yourself to uni."

"Yes. As I said before, my parents weren't poor. But my dad didn't make nearly enough to pay the tuition, or fees as you call them. I did well in school, though, and my grades got me a mostly full scholarship to Fordham, a Catholic university in New York. Every day, I'd take the ferry across the Hudson and then a train to the Bronx. "

"And you did well at Fordham and got a scholarship to Manchester?"

"Pretty much. I'm impressed you remember."

"You're very memorable, Elsie Farrell."

And to how many women had he said those words? I pushed doubt aside and basked in the candlelight.

After the waiter cleared our plates, we ordered coffee and dessert. Then Alec held my hand across the table. His velvety eyes were thoughtful.

"I suppose their coming to see you is out of the question."

"Yes, there's just not enough money to go around for plane tickets. It was hard being away from them on Christmas. I was mostly alone. Oh, I went to church with Mrs. Barrymore on Christmas Day."

"That sounds a dubious sort of comfort."

"It was nice to be honest. The congregation was welcoming."

"Are you religious, Elsie?"

I hesitated as I always did when people posed this question. I decided to answer honestly. I had nothing to lose after all.

"Not really. I was raised Catholic, and I don't consider myself Catholic, not anymore. But I believe in something—God, I suppose—and I like ritual. I don't go to church regularly, but I rather like knowing it's there. If that makes sense."

Alec nodded. "I know what you mean. I was brought up Church of England, and though I don't go to church myself, I like seeing churches and hearing bells ring and generally knowing they're there. If I went to see my mum, I'd go to church with her."

We smiled at each other as only two people who have finally found themselves understood can do.

The waiter appeared with our tiramisu and coffee. As I savored the liquor-soaked lady fingers, cocoa power, and whipped cream, I wondered again about Alec's relationship with his family. He seemed to be good terms with his mum. Why didn't he go home more often? Was there some tension with his dad or his brother? I decided against asking him.

After our meal, Alec helped me put on my coat. As we crossed the street, I shivered. He put his arm around my shoulder and drew me close. "We have a penchant for choosing the coldest nights, Elsie."

I nestled my head against his shoulder, grateful for the warmth and protection and conscious, even in the frigid air, of his musky scent.

In the car, he drew me to him. He kissed me, first gently, then, when I opened my mouth, harder. I tilted my head back, and his lips grazed my neck, covering it with small kisses.

"Elsie," he murmured, "Beautiful Elsie. Would you like some champagne?"

"Yes," I said simply. I hadn't expected the night to end like this, but somehow it felt right.

He kissed me again. His left held mine as we drove to the hotel.

With its Edwardian turrets and the light twinkling from its arched windows, the Midland managed to look simultaneously imposing and inviting. He parked in front of the entrance and handed his keys to a porter. His arm encircled my waist as we entered the lobby. For a moment, I felt self-conscious in front of the porter and the front desk clerk, but they seemed less interested in me than I was in them. In fact, they appeared not to see me at all.

In front of a large staircase, Alec paused. He glanced around in an exaggerated way as if to satisfy himself that we were alone. He placed a finger to his lips as if to silence me. Then he lifted me into his arms and carried me up one flight of stairs.

A giggle escaped me.

"Someone might hear you, and I can't very well shush you when I'm carrying you." But his velvety eyes smiled into mine.

The hallway was empty. In front of a door marked 226, he set me down. He unlocked the door .

"Come in," he murmured.

It was all the invitation I needed.

He took both of my hands, and we stepped into the room.

Thirteen

After that, Alec came to Manchester every week. Usually, he booked a room at the Midland for the weekend; occasionally he drove up on a weekday. Sometimes, we met my fellow lodgers or coursemates for a drink. But usually, the two of us had dinner together. Although we went other places, Isola Bella was our favorite restaurant. The proprietor, Mr. Evandro Barbieri himself, sometimes stopped by our table, and he and his staff addressed me as Miss Farrell. Although their deference made me want to giggle, I rather enjoyed being an important customer. Above all, it was our place. Sometimes, we went to the cinema or took bracing walks in the countryside outside Manchester.

Always, the evenings concluded in Alec's room in the Midland.

Mrs. Barrymore took my overnight sojourns better than I could have anticipated. Part of this I attributed to Ravi's deftness: his tale about Alec being a Royal Philharmonic violinist had removed much of Mrs. Barrymore's prejudice about his long hair. But much of it had to do with Alec himself. Every time he presented himself at the rowhouse, he had a small tribute for Mrs. Barrymore as well as for me, usually flowers, occasionally chocolates or fruit.

"Why, Mr. Wilder, you shouldn't have!" she'd exclaim. She'd beam at him and then race off to put the flowers in her best vase.

"Aren't you overdoing it a bit?" I asked one evening when Alec fetched me in his Mercedes. "I'm sure Mrs. Barrymore can see right through you. And even she's bound to weary of flowers eventually."

"Perhaps, but the reward is so worthwhile," he murmured. He kissed my hand and the inside of my wrist.

One Saturday morning in March, we lay in bed, my head on Alec's shoulder and his lean, strong arm around mine. It was nine o'clock, and we were thinking about breakfast. At least, I was. That, and how his arm felt around me.

"So you've let me into your world, Elsie," said Alec.

"My Manchester world. Slightly shabby, occasionally pretentious, and generally endearing. You've not been to Jersey City."

"Not yet, though I hope to. But it's about time I showed you my world."

My eyes widened. What exactly did he want to share with me? Wasn't this what Maggie had warned me about?

"I've seen you in concert," I said slowly. "And Lila and I went to the afterparty at the Piccadilly."

He bent forward and kissed me on the forehead. "Not my work, silly. My house in Kent. And it's about time you met my bandmates and friends. Properly, that is."

Lila and I had been introduced to Greg, the lead singer, at the concert's afterparty, but I couldn't say I'd met him properly.

"The Easter holidays are coming up," he continued. "What would you say to spending a week with me? We could drive down to my house and have the week there, maybe manage a day in London. And our producer's giving a party for the band and our crew that first Saturday. You could meet the band and their wives and girlfriends."

Wives and girlfriends. That meant he considered me his girlfriend.

"Yes, that would be lovely."

"Excellent." He gave my shoulders a squeeze. "It'll be fun to see what you make of my world."

Part of the duvet had fallen away, and I shivered.

"You're cold? I'll keep you warm."

Alec rolled onto me, and his dark eyes smiled into mine. We weren't having breakfast—not yet.

***

As the Easter holidays were fast approaching, it was natural we should discuss them in the postgraduate office. One damp Wednesday afternoon, after a lecture about Victorian narrators, Larry, Clara, and I huddled over cups of tea in one corner of the room. Across the room, Belle and Jules occupied a loveseat, his arm around her shoulder.

"I think Rogers and I will go back to Devon, at least for one weekend," said Larry. "If she can get off work."

Clara nodded. "That's my problem. Angie doesn't think she'll be able to take her holiday until later in the spring. Oh, well. If the weather's a bit better, we'll be able to take a walking holiday then, which is what we both want, really."

"I'm going to London over the hols," Jules announced. Ostensibly, he addressed Belle, but he spoke loudly enough so that we could hear him.

"Not pleasure, but business," he continued. "Rather a bore. Daddy knows some old publisher who's looking for a new editor. Apparently, he's willing to wait until I finish my degree. Anyhow, I might as well have lunch with the old man."

Belle giggled.

How had I ever, ever fancied him? Thought myself in love with him? Here he was, pretending to complain about a position that was being handed to him. I even felt sorry for Belle. For all her artistic pretensions, she was Manchester born and bred, and I knew she'd been the first in her family to finish her exams, much less contemplate university. His arrogance must be grating for her.

Clara rolled her eyes. "What are you doing over Easter, Elsie?"

"It looks as though I'll be spending the week with Alec. At his home in Kent."

I was conscious of Belle's and Jules' eyes on me. I didn't want to elaborate, but Larry and Clara were looking at me expectantly.

"He wants to show me his house and introduce me to his bandmates and crew," I said haltingly. "Apparently, there's going to be a sort of pre-tour party."

"Oh, the pre-tour party," said Belle as if she attended one every weekend. I immediately withdrew any sympathy I had for her.

"Well, that's lovely, pet," said Clara. "He's a good bloke, and I hope his bandmates are as nice as he is."

Larry nodded. "Very nice bloke."

"The thing about this publisher is that he doesn't understand that the last twenty years have transpired," Jules said. "He thinks the public still wants country house mysteries and spy novels—Agatha Christie and John Le Carré and such."

It was if the conversation had never touched on my plans.

Belle tittered. "That kind of publisher."

"And that kind of future editor," muttered Clara.

Even Larry permitted himself a smile.

My news wasn't as well received in Jersey City. In our world, nice women didn't go away with men who weren't their husbands.

Maggie was silent when I told her I would be spending the week with Alec in Kent. Though she said nothing, I could hear her misgivings. She was imagining me embarking on a career of drug addiction, punctuated, perhaps, by orgies.

"Well, you'll see another part of England," she said. "That will be something."

My mother took the news only slightly better.

"Oh!" she said when I told her.

"Yes," I replied in what I hoped was a matter-of-fact tone. "He wants to show me his house in Kent. And he's taking me to a party his producer is giving for the band and crew. I'll meet his bandmates and their wives and girlfriends."

"Oh!" she uttered again.

Then she seemed to realize she'd lapsed into monosyllables. "Well, that will be nice. He must really want you to meet them." She spoke in the brittle, animated voice she used when she wanted to convey more enthusiasm than she felt.

Nana was the worst precisely because she made an even grander attempt to feign approbation.

When I told her about the holiday in Kent, I heard a small, almost imperceptible gasp on the other end. I marveled at the technology that allowed someone in Manchester to hear a gasp in Jersey City.

She quickly collected herself. "He is a very generous man! He buys dinner and drinks for your friends, and now you will meet his friends. It is very exciting, Elsa."

For a moment, the line was silent. "I hope you will be careful, dear," she said finally.

Fourteen

Alec and I departed for Kent on Good Friday afternoon.

"Let me know how it goes," said Lila when she bade me farewell in the upstairs corridor. Her kohl-rimmed grey eyes glinted mischievously.

"And you enjoy your week with "Aunt Harriet.""

Impulsively, I gave her a hug, which she returned rather awkwardly. Her makeup and mummy research might be exotic, but her reserve was endearingly English.

Mrs. Barrymore insisted on seeing me off at the front door. She struck a dignified pose in her pumps and glasses.

"Goodbye, Miss Farrell," she said. "I hope you enjoy your time with Mr. Wilder's friends."

I'd told her we'd been invited to visit some of Alec's musical friends, which was true. She chose to believe that we were sleeping in separate beds under their roof.

"I've forgotten something in my car," said Alec suddenly. "Wait a moment."

In a moment, he reappeared with a bouquet of yellow carnations.

"Happy Easter, Mrs. Barrymore," he said, proffering them with a smile.

"Well, it's not Easter yet, but they're lovely," said Mrs. Barrymore gruffly. "Now you get on so that I can put these in water."

"She took that rather well," said Alec once we were inside the car. He raised my hand to his lips.

"I think she even bought that bit about forgetting the flowers."

"What's a little deception when you're what's at stake?" He kissed me gently on the lips and smiled into my eyes.

"I'd like to call my family on Easter," I said once we were on the motorway. "My parents and my nana and my sister. Just to say 'Happy Easter.' I wouldn't talk too long."

"You can talk as much as you like. There's enough in the kitty to cover a few transatlantic calls."

"What's Easter like in your family then?" he asked a few minutes later.

"Nice," I replied. "Simple. We decorate eggs on Easter Saturday, go to church Sunday morning, and then have a big family dinner on Sunday afternoon. Ham usually. And chocolate bunnies in the morning, of course."

"Lovely," he said, and I could tell he meant it.

"How about your family?" Surely, I had a right to ask after all the time we'd spent together.

"Much the same as your family. Chocolate, church, and dinner. Only we usually have lamb, not ham. When my dad was with us, that is. I don't know what they'll do this year." He kept his eyes on the motorway.

"Oh," I said limply, "I didn't know. I'm sorry."

"You had no way of knowing. I haven't exactly been forthcoming about it."

Alec switched lanes, overtaking a red Ford Escort.

"My dad died of a heart attack last June," he continued. "I was on tour in Australia, of all places. I flew home for the funeral. I haven't been back to Yorkshire since."

"Not even Christmas?"

He shook his head. "I was in Tenerife." His tone did not invite further questions.

"So I'm excited to bring you home, Elsie," he said in his usual bantering tone. "It will be fun to have you there."

"You make me sound like a new toy. Or a kitten."

"Aren't you though?" He lifted my hand to his lips, grazing the inside of my wrist with his mouth.

My whole body was attuned to his touch. Although we'd spent quite a few nights together at the Midland, this would be our first under his roof.

"What's your house like?" I asked.

"Queen Anne. It was originally some aristocrat's hunting lodge, sold off in the late nineteenth century when the family's fortunes declined."

"You know, I haven't yet seen a stately home," I said. "I'd love to."

"I'm sure we can manage that in the coming week. There are a few properties in Kent worth visiting."

"I'd like that." I hadn't gone out with many guys who were interested in my wishes.

"In terms of this coming week, I was thinking we could spend a couple days at mine," said Alec. "Go to Mike's party and such. Then we could visit some stately homes, maybe spend a couple days in

London. I could show you some of my favorite spots; perhaps we could even see a show in the West End."

"That would be lovely. There are a couple museums I'd like to see. And the Tower."

"Excellent. And no need to work out an itinerary. We can be spontaneous. Unless you feel better with one, that is."

"I rather relish the idea of being frivolous and irresponsible for a few days. I am on holiday after all."

"Then I'll do my best to cultivate that side of you." Again, he lifted my wrist to his lips.

"I've asked Mrs. Hall to cook for us tonight," Alec continued. "She comes to clean about once a week, but she occasionally cooks for me as well. Her husband looks after my garden. Anyway, she's cooking a simple roast with Yorkshire pudding and carrots. I'll give you the grand tour. Once dinner is served, Mrs. Hall will bugger off, and I'll have you all to myself."

I felt as though I'd stepped into one of the gothic romances Maggie and I devoured when we were younger. I was the governess about to be ravished by the master at his hunting lodge. Of course, Alec had a northern accent, I was not a governess, and we'd already spent the last few weekends together.

"Well, Elsie, does that plan meet with your approbation?"

"Yes, it does."

He smiled a little triumphantly, and I slapped him.

"What was that for?" he asked, rubbing his arm.

"You looked smug."

"As would any man who had you to himself for a week."

It was almost dusk when the Mercedes turned off a country road onto a long driveway. At the end was a three-story brick house capped by a hipped roof with two dormer windows.

"There it is," he said almost shyly as we approached the house. "Foxgrove Lodge."

"That's its name?"

"A few generations ago when it was still in the family's hands. Previous owners dropped the name, but when I bought it two years ago, I decided to resurrect it. Out of respect to the family and because I liked the idea of owning a house with a name."

"But you don't hunt."

"God, no. I can just about shoot clay pigeons."

He pulled into the garage that was just past the house on the circular drive. Two other cars were parked there, a small red car and a larger grey one.

"I thought you lived alone," I said.

"I do, the Halls live out—oh, you mean the cars. The red one is the Aston Martin, and that's the Rolls. I take the Martin out sometimes in the summer. The Rolls is a convertible, so I save it for finer weather as well."

Carrying my suitcase in one hand and holding my hand in the other, Alec walked me to the front door. I was quiet. Somehow, the knowledge that he owned three expensive cars stunned me. This didn't seem like the Alec I knew.

I recollected myself. "This is really pretty. The house and the grounds."

"It's a fairly small garden," replied Alec, "but I'll look forward to showing it to you in daylight."

The front door opened, and a thin, grey-haired women smiled at us from the doorway.

"Good evening, Mr. Wilder," she said. "It's lovely to have you back."

"It's good to be back. Mrs. Hall, may I present Elsie Farrell? Elsie, Mrs. Hall."

We shook hands, and she smiled warmly at me.

"It's lovely to meet you, Miss Farrell. The roast won't be ready for an hour or so, so that'll give you some time to settle in."

Alec gave me a tour of the house. On the ground floor was a kitchen, a dining room, a drawing room, a billiards room with a snooker table, and a library. He seemed especially attached to this chamber with its wood-beamed ceiling and inlaid bookcases. A shaggy brown rug occupied a small pit in front of the fireplace, and on one end of the room was his stereo.

I scanned the titles on one shelf. John Fowles's *The French Lieutenant's Woman*, some books by Kingsley Amis, and a few John Le Carré novels.

"I see you're critiquing my literary taste," said Alec, joining me in front of the bookcase. "Does it meet with your approval?"

I nodded. "It does. I like John Fowles, and I rather enjoy spy thrillers. And mysteries now and then. I've never outgrown Agatha Christie though some of my coursemates would no doubt crucify me for admitting as much."

"I didn't know anyone could outgrow Mrs. Christie. And she and Mr. Le Carré are handy when I'm on tour and want something to read. But let me show you one of my prize possessions."

Taking my hand, he led me to another shelf. He withdrew a thick black tome from the shelf and presented it to me.

"*The Oxford Book of English Verse*," I said. "Lovely."

"Look inside."

There was an inscription on the inside cover:

Presented to Alec Wilder
Winner of the Year Seven Prize for English Literature
North Allerton Grammar School
May 1959

I smiled. "Well done." I knew he didn't show it to many people.

"So you see, it was inevitable I would meet someone like you."

Next, he showed me the second and third floors as the British called the first and second floors. There were five bedrooms, one of which he used to store his guitars. He seemed to have about twenty of these.

After the tour, we returned to the library. We sat on the sofa, his arm around me and my head on his shoulder.

A bright object on the coffee table caught my eye. It looked like a small silver tower. "What's that?" I asked.

"A table lighter."

I wrinkled my nose. "Why do you need one like that?" He rarely smoked.

Alec shrugged. "I bought it because I could, I suppose." He laughed. "Rather like those three cars parked in the garage."

It was hard to reconcile the Alec who bought luxury cars and silver lighters he didn't need with the one who treasured his school prize.

There was a knock at the door. "Dinner is served," called Mrs. Hall cheerfully.

Candelabra cast a soft glow over the dining room table. Mrs. Hughes had uncorked a bottle of cabernet sauvignon.

"Well, I'll leave you to it," she said, wiping her hands on her apron. "I'll come round tomorrow afternoon to do the washing up. Jim and I are just across the way if you need anything."

We thanked her, and Alec poured our wine.

"Santé," he said, smiling into my eyes.

Simple English food and red wine had never tasted so good. I'd never had proper Yorkshire pudding before. It was flaky and fluffy, the beef was juicy, and the gravy robust. I was hungrier than I realized and found myself eating second helpings of everything.

"So what do you do make of Mrs. Hall?" Alec asked.

"She seems nice. Warm."

"She certainly liked you."

"But she seems the sort who'd be kind to everyone."

"She most assuredly is not. Oh, she's civil to all, but she's let several of my friends see her disapproval. Most of my fellow musicians, in fact."

The wine flowed freely, and we laughed a great deal. When we had eaten our fill of beef and Yorkshire pudding, we each ate a slice of the Arctic Roll Mrs. Hall had thoughtfully placed in the freezer.

"My mom would love this," I said, admiring the artfully placed swirls of raspberry jam and vanilla ice cream.

"So would mine," said Alec. "In fact, I rather suspect that's what she'll be serving for pudding on Sunday."

I longed to ask him more about her, but I didn't want to ruin the moment.

After dinner, we withdrew to the library. In front of a fire, we uncorked another bottle of wine. We sat on the rug in the pit before the fireplace, and Alec filled both of our glasses. The wood crackled, and the firelight cast a rosy glow over the bookcases.

"So what will Mike's party be like?" I asked.

"Bacchanalian," replied Alec, throwing an arm around my shoulder. "Lots of wine, people snorting cocaine off naked bodies, that sort of thing."

He was being flippant, of course. Still, I knew that he took drugs sometimes though he wasn't addicted. I believed him when he said he preferred a few pints to any drug. But it was possible the party would be wild. Wasn't this what Maggie had warned me about?

Alec must have felt me stiffen, for he drew me toward him and kissed the side of my forehead.

"I'm just messing with you," he said. "It won't be very decadent. In fact, anyone looking for rock star excesses would be very disappointed. Mike is pretty straitlaced— in some respects anyway—so the band and crew will be on their best behavior. There's a chance someone may imbibe a bit too much, and you might smell some smoke that's not tobacco. And I won't be drinking very much, so anytime you want to leave, we will. Mike's all right, but I have no desire to spend a night under his roof. Not when I have you here with me."

He kissed me then, and the taste of the wine mingled with his own musky scent. He kissed my neck as he unbuttoned my dress, and I let my doubts fall away.

Fifteen

We might have begun the night in the library, but we ended it up-stairs in Alec's four-poster bed. That's where I woke the next morning.

I had always been an early riser, so I found myself stirring around six. As Alec was still sound asleep, I put on my bathrobe and walked to the window. The sun's rays peaked pink and golden over the horizon, casting a rosy glow over Alec's back garden. I glimpsed an in-ground pool, a patio with a picnic table and chairs, and a garden that looked as though it might contain rosebushes. A hedgerow enclosed the grounds.

Then I sat on the window seat to survey the room itself. I had taken in relatively little the previous evening. There was a rather bulky wardrobe beside the bed where Alec lay on his side, one pale shoulder exposed. His mouth was slightly open, which made him look oddly young and vulnerable. On the bedside table sat a copy of *The Hobbit*. I was pleased to see that he loved this world of dwarves and elves and wizards as much as I did; it was an unexpected side of Alec.

Opposite the bed was something between a desk and vanity—perhaps a male vanity would be an apt term if such a piece even existed. A small box stood atop the table; I couldn't quite tell what it was. I approached the table to get a better look.

It was a perfume package. Chanel No. 5.

For a minute, I stared at the box, trying to make sense of what I had just seen.

In the room in which I had spent the night with Alec was a gift he had purchased for another woman. It was displayed openly on the table; perhaps he had forgotten it was there. It was a stunt worthy of Jules, and the fact that I had been duped by both of them in the space of a few months said much about me. I was naïve, gullible. Men like them probably saw me coming a mile away. I smiled bitterly.

One thing was certain: I wouldn't remain in that room or house a second longer than I had to. I would get dressed, and then, when Alec chose to bestir himself, I would ask him, with great dignity, to drive me to the nearest rail station. Or perhaps the Halls would give me a ride. In any case, I could find my own way back to Manchester, thank you very much.

The first thing was to get dressed. As quietly as I could, I took my suitcase into the bathroom. I showered and donned a pair of flared jeans and an orange cardigan. I would appear just like any other student on the train. That's what I was, and I had been foolish to think any man, especially one like Alec, could see me otherwise.

Once I was dressed, I realized I had left my shoes in Alec's room. Despite my attempts to tiptoe into the room, the door creaked when I opened it.

Alec stirred. From the doorway, I saw him roll toward the sound. He opened his eyes and blinked at me.

"Why are you up so early, Elsie?" he asked. "I thought we were going to have a real lie-in."

"I—I wanted to get dressed," I said, "so that I could be on my way as quickly as possible." I tried to sound dignified, but my voice faltered.

He rubbed his eyes. "But we've got loads of time. The party's not till the evening."

Alec seemed genuinely confused. It was hard to reconcile this sleepy, slightly bewildered boy with the callous philanderer who displayed perfume for one woman in the same room where he bedded another.

All my resolve faltered. And yet I couldn't let the perfume go completely.

"There's Chanel No. 5," I said. Stupidly, I pointed to the bottle on the vanity.

Half sitting up in bed, Alec rubbed his eyes.

"Oh," he yawned, "that's for my mum. Her birthday's a few weeks off, so I picked some up when I was last in London. I'll post it when the time comes."

Still clutching my suitcase in one hand, I sank onto the window seat. I had nearly ended it all because of a gift for his mum.

"You all right, Elsie?"

I nodded. "Though I expect your mum would prefer it if you gave it to her in person." I hadn't meant to say that.

Alec smiled sleepily.

"As always, Elsie, you are right in all respects but one: being such an early riser. Come here."

I stood by the bedside. Alec tugged gently at my wrists until I sat on the bed. He kissed me and then surveyed me.

"You look beautiful in orange, Elsie," he said. "It's rather a shame it has to come off."

***

We didn't get out of bed until ten. After a breakfast of toast and fried eggs, Alec insisted on giving me a tour of the grounds.

The in-ground pool was beautiful, but I wrinkled my nose a little when he showed it to me.

"How often do you actually swim in it?" I asked.

He laughed. "There aren't a lot of days in an English summer that are warm enough for the pool or the seaside. I had the pool installed last spring. I probably managed six or seven days in it last summer."

Putting an arm around my shoulder, he drew me near and planted a kiss on my forehead. "Now that you're in my life, I'll make more use of it."

"That's the thing. I like swimming, but almost no pool is warm enough for me. Except on the hottest summer afternoons."

"Then I'll warm you up."

That afternoon, Alec attempted to teach me snooker. When that failed—after I succeeded in sending several balls onto the floor—we cuddled on the sofa in the library. Lying in his arms, I wondered how I could have overreacted to the perfume as I had. Then I surrendered to the pleasure of feeling Alec's arms around me.

When Mrs. Hall came round to do the washing up, I offered to help her. At first, she was startled, but she quickly accepted my offer. We chatted as she washed the dishes and I dried them. Then I attempted to put them away.

"I'm glad you're enjoying your time in Kent, Miss Farrell," she said. "What part of America did you say you're from? No, dear, the knives go there. In that drawer. Jersey City? I've not heard of it. Oh, it's near

New York City? No, dear, the glasses go there. In that cabinet. What would you like to see in Kent? Oh, you're in for a treat; Kent has some of the finest properties in the country. No, Miss Farrell, the dessert plates don't go on top of the bigger ones. Thank you for your help, but perhaps you should let me do it, my dear. Now why don't you go to the library and keep Mr. Wilder company?"

I kept a straight face. It was her job, after all.

Alec was stretched on the sofa when I returned to the library. "That was quick."

"Mrs. Hall didn't want my help. In fact, she summarily dismissed me." I recounted our exchange.

Alec's shoulders shook. "Still, I expect you've made a good impression. None of my guests have ever offered to help her. In fact, I'm not sure she'd even allow them over the kitchen threshold. I'd say you're on your way to becoming a favorite."

I dressed with care for the party, choosing a white belted mini dress with a pleated skirt I'd purchased from Dorothy Perkins earlier that week. It had seemed suitable, even trendy, in the light of the store's changing room that Wednesday. But as I surveyed myself in the bathroom mirror, I appeared younger than I was, a girl playing at glamor with cheap cosmetics and high street knockoffs. The musicians' wives were sure to sport the latest fashions from London boutiques. I'd never cared much about brand names before, and neither did anyone else in my circle, apart from Maggie when we were younger. If I liked something and it suited me and I could afford it, I bought it. Now, at the thought of meeting the band members' wives, I suddenly felt self-conscious about my dress.

Alec did a great deal to restore my confidence.

"Wow!" he said when I entered the library. He rose from the sofa.

I stood before him, and he kissed me, gently at first and then more urgently.

"You look beautiful, Elsie," he murmured. "Now I find I don't want to go out after all. Let's give Mike his due and then come straight home."

"So who exactly is going to be there tonight?" I asked as we drove to the party in the Rolls Royce.

"The band—Greg, Billy, and Dave. Greg's wife, Betty, and Billy's, Irene. Dave's girlfriend Mandy should be there as well. Now that I think of it, they're engaged now. Some of the crew should be there, too, with or without lady friends. You remember Lucas?"

"It'll be nice to see him again." I was relieved there would be a familiar face at the gathering.

"He's a good bloke. And Mike and his wife will be hosting, of course, though she's probably in France at the moment." He paused. "And our opening act will probably be there as well."

Mike's house was about a forty-five-minute drive from Foxgrove Lodge. It proved to be a red brick Georgian manor.

"Small as manor houses go, large as houses go," remarked Alec as the Rolls turned into a long driveway. "Our producers live rather better than we do."

"And you live better than most."

"An excellent reminder." He kissed my hand.

As we pulled into the circular drive in front of the house, I again felt as though I were entering an earlier time, one of great houses and balls and candlelight chandeliers. I half expected to be greeted by a servant in livery and to see women in ballgowns and men in top hats.

A man answered our knock at the front door. I recognized him as the huge Irishman who'd summoned Lila and me to the party after the concert.

"Good evening, Sean," said Alec.

"Good evening, Alec, Miss Farrell. They're all in the drawing room if you want to go through."

"Does he work for Mike, too?" I whispered after we stepped into the hallway. It was hard to imagine this Irish giant as a manservant.

Alec shook his head. "No, I expect Mike just hired him for tonight. For security."

No butler then. Alec took my hand and led me into a large hallway. As I would have expected, artwork adorned the walls. However, instead of the solemn portraits I would have imagined, abstract paintings and pop art greeted me.

The drawing room was a large room flanked by round arches and illuminated by electric chandeliers. Large plants flanked its corners, and a small orange tree occupied a small recess in the floor. People chatted in small groups, some of them clustered by a table that seemed to promise refreshments.

A plump, smiling man hastened toward us. "Hello, Alec, aren't you going to introduce us?" His small bright eyes moved over me appraisingly, but not unkindly.

"Elsie, this is Mike Harmony, our host and the one who makes sure our records are palatable. Mike, may I present Elsie Farrell?"

I extended my hand, and Mike kissed it, his lips lingering just a fraction longer than was necessary on my fingers.

"A pleasure, Elsie. Thank you so much for gracing my home."

Alec frowned slightly. "Oh, there's Lucas." One hand on my arm, he steered me toward his friend.

Just a few months earlier, I wouldn't have dreamed of being invited to a house like this, let alone being greeted as a guest of honor by its owner. Mike's admiration was flattering, if disconcerting, but Alec's proprietary hand reassured me. He wouldn't have reacted to Mike's overtures that way if he hadn't considered me his girlfriend.

While Alec wore his blue velvet sport coat, Lucas, I noticed, had not dressed for the occasion. He sported jeans and a denim jacket over a white tee shirt that said "Southampton F.C." His attire contrasted with the room's graceful proportions and the curved wineglass he held in one hand.

Lucas seemed genuinely pleased to see me. It was hard to believe he had been so grumpy at the concert's afterparty.

"Lovely to see you again, my dear," he said. "Tell Lila Pam will ring her soon about the Egyptology museum."

So that at least had been real.

"Is Pam here tonight?" I asked.

Lucas shook his head. "She couldn't get away from uni. Well, it's the Easter holidays, but you know what I mean. Pressure of work and such."

"I look forward to meeting her when she comes to Manchester."

He smiled. "Perhaps we can all go out for a pint or a bite then."

"Speaking of pints and bites, I'm thirty and hungry," said Alec. "Let's get some food and something to wet our whittle."

The sideboard held trays of cheese and prawn cocktails and tiny sausage rolls. We filled our plates, and Mike made a great show of asking me what I wanted to drink. He ceremoniously poured a glass of Chablis and handed it to me.

We stood nibbling our hors d'oeuvres, or starters as the British called them, and sipping our drinks.

"And now the band is approaching," said Alec ironically.

The three musicians and their fair ladies indeed seemed to be advancing toward us. The men were dressed in much the same way as Alec in their colorful sport coats, and the women looked fashionable.

A tall, dark-haired girl in a white tunic pantsuit walked beside Greg, the blond singer. The bearded bassist had his arm around a slight woman in a silver bodysuit under an open black skirt; she wore her light brown hair in round buns on either side of her head. And the mustachioed drummer held hands with a blond girl in a pink and green floral-patterned dress with bell sleeves.

In their very different ways, all three women looked elegant. My confidence waned. I wished that Alec and I could spend the evening chatting to Lucas or, better yet, that we had never left Foxgrove Lodge.

"Alec, mate, introductions are in order," said the one I recognized as Billy, the bearded bassist.

And so, Alec introduced me to his bandmates and their ladies. If Greg, the blond singer, recognized me from the party at the Piccadilly, he evinced no sign of it. They all shook hands with me and smiled pleasantly.

"So, how long have you been putting up with Alec?" asked Greg.

"Just about three months," Alec replied for me.

"I'm sure it feels longer to her," said Dave, the drummer with the droopy mustache.

Everyone laughed, and the ice, if there had been any, was broken. We split in two with the men forming one circle and the women another.

"Where in the States are you from?" asked Betty, the brunette in the white trouser suit.

"Jersey City. Just across the river from New York City."

"Do you get into the city much?" asked Irene, Billy's wife. "When you're at home, I mean."

"Sometimes. I used to take the ferry every day when I was at uni, and sometimes, my sister and I go to New York for the day."

"I thought you sounded like you were from New York," said the blond, Mandy, smiling. "Not that I'm an expert on American accents, mind."

Although all three women were attractive, Mandy was the most striking of the trio with her blond hair and warm brown eyes. She was curvaceous with round, slightly childlike features. A slight gap between her front teeth only added to her charm.

"But your accents are so much more interesting than ours," I replied.

Irene snorted. "Not mine! I'm a Bromie."

We talked a bit where they were from, where I'd been in England, and where we lived now. Within five minutes, I found it hard to believe I had ever found the prospect of meeting them intimidating. Apart from their fashionable clothes, they seemed like girls I might meet in a Manchester shop or even in Jersey City.

Behind us, a door slammed. Startled, I jerked my head around. A woman, or perhaps a girl, entered the drawing room in a short green dress. She moved swiftly, swinging her shoulders, so her blond hair bounced as she walked. Just behind her, a man walked quickly as if he were trying to keep up with her.

'Oh, God, Cheryl," Betty muttered, rolling her eyes and exhaling cigarette smoke at the ceiling.

"Who's Cheryl?" I asked.

"An absolute nightmare," replied Irene in a hushed voice.

The pair stopped by the sideboard to get a drink and then they strode toward our group. Or rather, the woman did; the man stayed a pace or two behind her, almost deferentially.

Somehow—I was never quite sure how afterward—the two sub-groups, male and female, merged again. It reminded me of something about cellular reproduction from high school biology. Alec, I noticed, had left his bandmates. He was chatting with Lucas and the other roadies in another corner of the room.

"Hello, everyone!" said Cheryl brightly when she joined our group. She was petite, about my height, and she would have been strikingly pretty if not for the hardness in her green eyes.

"Hi, Cheryl, Rick, you all right," said Greg. He sounded completely disinterested in her answer.

There was a hum as the musicians and their ladies echoed his greetings.

"I'm fine, and so is Rick," she replied. "Aren't you, Rick?"

"Yes." The man behind her nodded swiftly. He would have been quite nice-looking if his hazel eyes hadn't been wide and fearful.

"So we haven't all met," she said. "Isn't someone going to do the introductions?" Her voice was warm, but her green eyes narrowed as they met mine. Perhaps I looked like an imposter in my Dorothy Perkins dress.

"Elsie, this is Cheryl Wiles, who is supporting us on our upcoming tour," said Billy. "And this is Rick Brickson whose voice you might recognize if you ever watch tennis on telly. Cheryl and Rick, meet Elsie Farrell, Alec's girlfriend."

"Elsie's very clever," said Mandy. "She's doing a master's in English literature at Manchester Uni."

She spoke of me the way people talked about shy children. Perhaps she felt sorry for me in my high street dress.

"Lovely to meet you," said Rick, shaking my hand. "Your course sounds jolly interesting."

"So does your work," I said. "I like to watch tennis."

Cheryl shook my hand limply.

"Well, I wouldn't say I was supporting Serval. Serval is supporting me, really." Thus, she disposed of Serval's pretensions, her friend's career, and my academic ambitions.

"Are you a singer?" I asked politely.

Her eyebrows shot up. "Do I sing?" She broke into song, singing the chorus from a pop song in a surprisingly light, sweet voice. The lyrics and tune were vaguely familiar.

"Oh, I've heard that before," I said. "You can really sing."

She tossed her hair and smiled. "So you see, Serval should support me. The entire band."

Greg lit a cigarette. "But you've got your own band, Cheryl. You don't need us."

"The guitarist is new. I don't know if he'll work out."

"Remember that time we hired the keyboardist in Copenhagen," said Dave. "He sounded all right in the studio."

Billy laughed loudly. "And right before the show, he showed up barely able to stand. So we did without a keyboard part on "Jungle." Fortunately, the fans didn't seem to notice. I still don't know what he was on."

He laughed again, and everyone laughed with him. Everyone that is, except for Cheryl and Rick. Rick looked terrified and Cheryl stone-faced.

Cheryl tossed her hair again. "Well, if anything happens to my guitarist, I fully expect Alec to step in."

She cast a challenging glance in my direction. Did things happen to guitarists on tour? What precisely did she expect me to do about her guitarist or Alec?

"Well, I could do with a few more of these cheesy things," said Mandy. "Come with me, Elsie." She linked her arm with mine and drew me away from the group.

And so I found myself at the sideboard with Mandy. She filled her plate, and I followed suit.

"I'll take a few more of these prawns and these olives and these cheesy bits. I love food; Dave tells me if I keep at it, I'll be fat before I'm thirty." She popped an olive between her orange lips. "So what do you think of it all, love?"

"What do you mean?"

"The party, everything." She gestured vaguely as if to encompass the entire room.

"It's lovely. Everyone's been really kind."

"They are, aren't they? I remember how nervous I was when Dave first took me to a do like this last year when we started going out. I agonized over what to wear. But Irene and Betty are so down-to-earth. You know, none of us grew up going to houses like this. I'm a hairdresser, Betty worked in a shop before she married Greg, and Irene was a typist. And all the blokes had ordinary jobs before Serval took off. You're the posh one with your master's degree."

She smiled, and I realized she was trying to reassure me. I also noticed she didn't mention Cheryl.

"Oh, there's nothing remotely posh about my background," I said. "How about Cheryl?"

"I don't know her all that well," she said vaguely. "None of us do, really. What do you think of Manchester, then?"

Out of the corner of my eye, I saw Cheryl, trailed by Rick, approach the small circle, where Alec was chatting with the crew. She spoke to him, he replied, and he shook hands with Rick. Then, he moved toward the sideboard, smiling at me.

He put an arm around my waist and drew me close. "Has Mandy been telling you tales about us?" he asked lightly.

"Only how lovely and friendly everyone is," I replied.

"When we're on our best behavior, that is," said Dave, who had appeared at Mandy's elbow. He squeezed her shoulder with one hand.

"Which you are definitely not at home."

"Just because I didn't do the washing up when you were at your mum's—"

"And you didn't clean the cat's box."

"Isn't that what you're for?" But his blue eyes softened as they rested on Mandy.

"Speaking of home, Elsie and Alec should come to ours for a little dinner party," said Mandy. "When the tour is over."

I was being invited to another band member's house. And since Alec had often spoken of Dave as his best mate in the band, it must mean the band regarded me as Alec's girlfriend.

Dave fidgeted with his mustache. "If Elsie manages to civilize him between now and then. The way things stand, I don't know that I'd want Alec eating opposite me at my dining room table."

"Between Elsie and Mrs. Hall, I may join civilization as early as this summer," said Alec. "Just serve simple fare— fish and chips or egg and chips and lots of napkins—and I should be all right."

Next, Alec introduced me to the crew. As we chatted with them and Lucas, Cheryl watched us narrowly from across the room. For some reason, the woman disliked me immensely. I wondered if I had offended her when I hadn't recognized her name. Or perhaps she was just a difficult person. Betty and Irene had certainly suggested as much. I resolved to ask Alec about her.

Alec kissed my forehead. "I'm knackered. Want to call it a night?"

"Yes." The party had been less nerve-wracking than I had imagined, but I would be happy to return home, that is, to Foxgove Lodge.

Before we left, we said goodbye to other guests with the exception of Cheryl and Rick, who had adjourned to another room.

Mandy smiled warmly when we parted. "It would be lovely to see you again, love. Maybe you could get down to London and we could go shopping."

"I'd like that." I liked Mandy for her own sake, and it was flattering that the drummer's fiancée wanted to see me again.

"How'd you enjoy the party?" asked Alec as the Rolls Royce headed down the circular drive.

"Better than I expected. Everyone was lovely, especially Mandy."

"She's a sweetheart, isn't she? I'm glad you got on with her."

"That singer, Cheryl—she behaved kind of strangely," I said hesitantly.

"Did she? Well, you know what they say about the artistic temperament."

We turned onto the main road. For a few minutes, we drove in silence. Then Alec cleared his throat.

"So I know we talked about spending the week in Kent, maybe going to London one day," he said. "But what would you say to a change of plans?"

"What were you thinking?" Did this have anything to do with Cheryl or the party?

"North Yorkshire. I've given some thought to what you said about seeing my mum. I owe her a visit, and I'd like you to meet her."

Sixteen

"Yes," I said. "I'd like that."

"You're certain? I know we talked about visiting some stately homes and spending a day in London—" Alec sounded genuinely concerned.

"This is more important," I said quietly.

"Thank you, Elsie." He kissed my hand.

That morning, I'd been persuaded he was using me, that he was buying Chanel No. 5 for another woman even as he bedded me. Now he was inviting me to meet his mother. Wasn't that the ultimate sign of a man's interest?

Above all, Alec wanted to see his mother again. Although he clearly loved her, something had been keeping him away. I wasn't quite sure what it was, but at least it was no longer keeping them apart.

"When will we go to Yorkshire?" I asked finally.

"Sunday afternoon—if it's convenient for Mum. Part of me wants to drive up tomorrow morning, but Mum will probably have Peter and his family round for tea. I wouldn't want to disrupt their plans."

Alec's tone gave it away: it was Peter or something about him that was keeping him from home. I wouldn't ask him about it. Not yet anyway.

"What will we do Easter morning then?" I asked.

Alec threw an arm around my shoulder. "Wouldn't you like to know?"

When I awoke the next morning, the other side of the bed was empty. Alec had probably gone to the bathroom. Soon, he would return, and I would be in his arms. I yawned and snuggled under the duvet.

But Alec didn't return. I turned over. This wasn't like him. He was not an early riser, and we hadn't gotten to sleep until around one.

What if something were wrong? For all I knew he might be unconscious in the bathroom, not that we'd had very much to drink the previous night.

I rose and donned my dressing gown. I tried one upstairs bathroom, then another. No Alec. Slowly, I walked downstairs. This was strange.

The library was empty as were the drawing and billiard rooms. The house was quiet; there was no noise of a radio or television to suggest human presence. The only sound was a magpie calling in the back garden.

Surely, he wouldn't have run an errand without leaving a note. For one wild moment, I wondered if he had tired of me and left. I shoved that misgiving aside: he had just declared that he wanted me to meet his mum.

Finally, I pushed open the kitchen door. "Are you all right?" I called.

"Why shouldn't I be all right?"

Alec sat at the kitchen table in his dressing gown, his hands around a blue beaker. He smiled sleepily at me. A small cowlick stood up at the back of his head; I wanted to smooth it.

"I woke up, and you weren't there," I said feebly. I couldn't believe I had briefly suspected him of abandoning me.

"Because I was here drinking coffee, silly. Would you like some?"

"Tea, please."

"I'll put the kettle on. Now close your eyes."

"When can I open them?"

"When I say so."

I kept my eyes shut tight. There was the sound of running water and then the clatter of the kettle on the hob.

"You can open them."

On the table before me was a black and silver box with the logo of a posh London store. Inside it was a smaller box with the same logo. One side was plastic, and behind it was the largest chocolate egg I had ever seen. It was wrapped in silver foil, and according to the picture on the box, the silver orb was a dark chocolate egg that held dozens of tiny dark chocolate eggs, all wrapped in foil of their own.

"Oh!" I exclaimed. "I've never seen anything like this before."

"Then come here and thank me properly."

I stood before him, and he pulled me gently onto his knee. His dark eyes smiled into mine. I put my arms around his neck, and he kissed me slowly. "Happy Easter, Elsie."

We spent a quiet morning lounging around the house, reading and watching telly. Around midday, we walked to the nearest pub for a Sunday roast. To my surprise, neither the landlord nor the other patrons seemed particularly interested in Alec. We might have been any couple having a pint and bite at the local. They were far more immersed in their game of darts.

I shared this observation with Alec as we walked home.

"You forget that all of my fans are under thirty and most of them are under twenty-five," he replied. "To the locals over thirty, I'm just the longhaired bloke who bought Foxgrove Lodge. They'll leave me alone as long as I behave myself."

"Really," he continued, "it's a bit of a relief to be anonymous or nearly so, especially when I just want my girl to myself."

After our meal, I called Jersey City to wish my family a happy Easter. We left Foxgrove Lodge in the Rolls Royce at half past one. The drive to North Yorkshire would take about six hours, and Alec had promised his mum we'd arrive around seven or a little after.

"Of course, she would have been overjoyed to have us for Easter dinner," he said as we got onto the motorway. "She said as much when I rang this morning."

"Then why didn't we drive up this morning?"

"We had our own plans."

My chocolate egg and a pub roast. If his mum would have been so pathetically glad to welcome him home for the holiday, it seemed churlish not to go, whatever was between him and his brother.

He seemed to read my thoughts. "And it would have thwarted theirs. Well, Peter's. He and Jennie and the kids would be round for dinner, and I doubt my presence would have added to his enjoyment of the feast. Quite the reverse."

So this was it.

"In fact, I suspect I spoiled his mutton anyway," Alec continued. "If I know Mum, she'll have made much of my homecoming. That alone would ruin Easter for Peter. It might have been better to ring Mum after tea."

"But if he reacts like that, surely that's his problem," I said slowly.

Alec nodded quickly. "Yes. And no. Peter resents me; he always has. But his feelings aren't entirely unjustified."

For a few minutes, we drove in silence, Alec tight-lipped staring at the motorway, me stealing occasional glances at him out of the corner of my eye. Perhaps I would finally hear the whole story.

"When we were lads, I was Mum's favorite," he said finally. "It didn't matter so much then, at least to me, because Peter was Dad's. It worked out quite neatly. We both got plenty of love, and we were both someone's favorite. To me, it all felt very comfortable.

"We got older. We took our turns running about the football pitch, and we helped Dad in his garage. It was his wish that both of us would follow him into the business. Peter liked the work and had a real aptitude for it, me less so. I did well at school, so there was talk of me going to university. Mum had a habit of telling people how clever I was, and that got to Peter. All very understandable.

"I did A levels. I started them anyway. But music proved a bigger draw than literature or history or languages. Soon, I was skipping lectures to play gigs. Mum and Dad got wind of this, and though they were not pleased, they accepted it when I left school to pursue music full time. They wanted my happiness even more than they wanted a son at university.

"Then there were the years when I was a milkman during the day and then played gigs at night. They were relieved I was gainfully employed. But then Serval took off. They didn't love the music—Dad especially was clear about that—but they were proud of me. Mum put newspaper clippings about me in the family bible. Dad displayed some in the garage so that customers could see them.

"I think I mentioned I was on tour in Australia when Dad died. I came home for the funeral, and after the service, when people came round for a luncheon, Peter had a go at me. He said I had brought the heart attack on Dad, first by not following him into the business, then by not finishing A levels, and finally by worrying him with what Peter called my hedonistic lifestyle. Or maybe he said selfish. In any case, we had words, and he told me he never wanted to see me again. I don't know what I said. I think I called him a self-righteous prick.

"Anyway, the result is that we haven't seen each other since the funeral—and I haven't seen Mum since then either. I know Peter still means what he said. But I also know that he holds the fact I haven't seen Mum against me. I can't win."

"You're the prodigal son," I said slowly.

"Exactly. And Peter is still a self-righteous prick. But on some level, he's right."

"But you didn't cause your father's heart attack! He can't accuse you of that."

"No. Dad had high blood pressure, had had it for years. But having me for a son didn't help."

He stared stonily ahead, his mouth set firmly.

That was the reason he didn't want to speak of home, the reason he'd spent Christmas in Tenerife. Guilt. And his more recent regrets about avoiding his mother only compounded his remorse.

"But you're going home now," I said quietly. "That's a step."

"Yes, Elsie. And all because of you."

He smiled, and taking my hand, he raised it to his lips.

Seventeen

We arrived in Reston at around seven. Just as dusk settled on the village, we drove through the small market square.

"Reston is one of the few villages in North Yorkshire that still has a shop," said Alec. "There's a pub that does quite well and a post office. We've got a primary school though how long that will last is anyone's guess."

"And a chapter of Cats Protection," I added.

Alec grinned. "Thanks to my mum."

On the outskirts of the village, the Rolls stopped outside a two-story cottage flanked by two chimneys. As soon as the car halted, an outside light came on, and the door opened.

A small woman beamed from the doorway, illuminated by the light in the foyer behind her. Two cats, a slim tabby and a plump tuxedo, curled around her legs. They seemed extensions of her.

As we approached, I saw she had thick dark hair, which she wore in an outgrown bob, and warm brown eyes. Although her smile took in both of us, she had eyes only for Alec.

"Happy Easter, Alec," she said. "I don't know whether to scold you for being late or for driving too quickly with that poor lass in the car." Her tone was light, but her eyes were moist.

"Reprimand me on both accounts, Mum."

Alec kissed her cheek and enveloped her in a hug. For a few minutes, he held her tightly. Then she pushed him away, laughing lightly. A tear streaked her cheek.

"My, but we're a soppy pair. Now you mind your manners, Alec Wilder, and introduce me to this lovely girl."

"Mum, this is Elsie Farrell. Elsie, my mum."

I smiled and extended my hand. "It's lovely to meet you, Mrs. Wilder."

A small hand clasped mine, and her eyes, so like Alec's, crinkled at the corners. "It's a pleasure to meet you, Miss Farrell. Do come in."

We stepped into a tiny hall. I knelt to greet the cats. The tabby warmed to me instantly, rubbing her head against my thigh. The tuxedo cat gazed at me with round green eyes and sniffed my finger cautiously before brushing her velvety nose against it.

"Can you introduce me to the cats?" I asked.

"Well, it seems as though you're already on good terms with them, but the tabby is Alice, and the tuxedo is My Lady. She's usually timid, My Lady is, but she's taken a liking to you. Now I'll show you both where you'll be staying and then you come to the kitchen for some shepherd's pie. It's nearly ready."

"Oh, Mum, you didn't have to cook—" Alec began.

Mrs. Wilder snorted. "And have you and Miss Farrell come all that way and no tea? Don't be ridiculous. You can go to your old room, and I'll show Miss Farrell Peter's room, where she'll be staying."

We followed Mrs. Wilder up a narrow staircase, Alec carrying both our suitcases.

"I hope you don't mind sharing a room with cats, my dear," she continued. "I'm boarding two at the moment, a dear old ginger tom in Alec's room and a little black cat and her kittens in the room where you'll be sleeping. Our chapter doesn't have a shelter yet, so we board the cats where we can. I'd give 'em the run of the house, but my Alice is a bit of a tartar where other cats are concerned. She accepts My Lady because My Lady was here first, but woe betide any imposters. So the boarders are each confined to one room, poor things. Still, I expect it's for the best as they get a bit of security after all they've been through."

"I'd love to share my room with cats," I said. "I miss my own."

"Very good of you to say so, my dear. Here's your room. It's not changed much since Peter, my eldest, left home, about ten years ago. I hope you don't mind."

She opened the door, ushered me in, and closed the door hurriedly behind us as she flicked a light switch.

"I just can't risk Cleo getting out or Alice getting in," she said apologetically.

The room was small, about the same size as mine at Mrs. Barrymore's house. Like my bedchamber at Mrs. Barrymore's, it held a narrow bed, a nightstand, a desk, and a small wardrobe. A Leeds Football Club poster bedecked one wall, and yellowed newspaper clippings about footballers covered another. A cardboard box occupied one corner of the room, and tiny mews escaped it.

"This is cozy," I said and meant it. "Thank you so much for having me at such short notice."

"Of course, you're very welcome, my dear. Cleo's very friendly and loves to be stroked, but she can be a bit touchy about her kittens, so I should leave them alone and her too when she's in the box. If she comes out of the box, though, you can make much of her. Now just come down when you're ready."

A few minutes later, the three of us were sat around the long table in Mrs. Wilder's kitchen. She spooned steaming mashed potatoes, carrots, peas, and minced beef, all covered in gravy, onto our plates. She drank an orange squash herself, but opened a bottle of red wine for us.

"This is delicious," I said. I hadn't realized how ravenous I was until I smelled the gravy and potatoes.

"Well, it isn't much, my dear. I wish you'd come earlier. We had a proper Easter dinner with roast lamb and minty peas and pudding."

My eyes flitted to Alec. He was frowning into his mash.

"But this is so good," I said. "Comfort food."

"Comfort food?" Mrs. Wilder's dark eyebrows met over her small nose.

"In the States, that's what we call our favorite foods, the ones that remind us of us home and that we enjoy when we're feeling low. Macaroni and cheese, grilled cheese, mash, that sort of thing."

Mrs. Wilder nodded thoughtfully. "Yes, I can see that. And shepherd's pie was Alec's favorite when he was a boy, so I suppose it's his comfort food. I hope so anyway! Now, tell me, dear, where in the States are you from?"

Alec's eyes met mine, he smiled, and his shoulders relaxed palpably. At least, I'd been able to avert a possible argument.

The three of us chatted easily for the rest of the meal. Then, Mrs. Wilder, her dark eyes sparkling, rose from her seat. She darted into refrigerator and emerged with a round glass casserole. Beaming, she bore it to the table.

"The Queen's pud!" said Alec. "Mum, you do too much." But he was smiling.

"It's my kitchen, Alec Wilder, and you are not the boss of me. Besides, it was easy enough to throw together."

The Queen's pudding proved to be a bread pudding topped with meringue and strawberry jam. It was scrumptious, and I told Mrs. Wilder so. But even while I praised her cooking, I couldn't help thinking that the woman must have spent the whole day in the kitchen, preparing two Easter dinners, one for each of her sons. She had gone to all this trouble for them and, by extension, me.

"So, initially, Mum, our plan was to spend the week in Kent," said Alec. "I promised Elsie I'd show her some stately homes, and we talked of going down to London for a day—"

Mrs. Wilder put her spoon down. "You promised this girl a week of proper sightseeing, and then you took her to see your old mother in Yorkshire? I've a mind to cuff you round the ears."

"Let me finish, Mum. So now that we find ourselves in North Yorkshire, I thought the three of us might take in some of the local sites. You could play tourist in your own county. Since Elsie's keen to see some stately homes, I reckon we could visit—"

"Mount Grace Priory!" exclaimed Mrs. Wilder.

"Yes, Mum, And then we might grab a bite at—"

"Betty's Tea Rooms," finished Mrs. Wilder. "There's a lovely café in Northallerton now, so it's not as if we'd even need to drive to York or Harrogate. They've got the nicest cakes and pastries."

She clasped her hands and smiled so merrily so that she appeared girlish despite the crow's feet around her eyes and the grey hairs near her temples.

"That's one thing you'll notice about my mum," remarked Alec. "She always interrupts, and she fancies herself a mind reader. Sometimes, she even gets it right."

"Listen to that cheek," she muttered. But her eyes were soft.

***

The next day, the three of us visited Mount Grace Priory. It proved to be a Georgian mansion on the grounds of what had once been a Carthusian priory. Although the priory itself had been ravaged during the dissolution of the monasteries during the reign of Henry VIII, its ruins remained. The house contained an exhibit about daily life at the monastery, and our docent seemed more eager to discuss the monks' world than he was the family who had occupied the estate after the priory closed.

After our tour, we strolled about the gardens. The day was warm for late April, and the three of us sat on a stone bench. Insects buzzed around us, and the sun felt pleasantly warm on my neck.

"Of course, I can remember when there was still a family at the great house," said Mrs. Wilder. "Not at Mount Grace, of course, but at Wexley Manor, just outside Reston. Things weren't what they used to be by then; the family made do with a skeleton staff. After the war, Sir Jason sold the manor. It's been an old people's home ever since."

She sighed. "Change is inevitable, and sometimes, it's for the best. Still, it's sad to see the old ways die. In any case, it's nice the manor's still there. It's lovely to see it there, and the nurses and carers bring some custom to the village. So many villages have lost their great houses and shops and schools. . ."

"In any case," Mrs. Wilder continued, "we've got a stately home-owner in the family now."

"Hardly, Mum. It's a little hunting box."

"A little hunting box! You make it sound like a snare for some poor rabbit. See how grand my son has become, Miss Farrell? I rely on you to keep him in check."

Afterward, we had tea at Betty's Tea Rooms.

"We could start with smoked salmon and cucumber sandwiches," said Mrs. Wilder doubtfully as she surveyed the menu.

"Or we could go straight to the sweeties," I said.

Mrs. Wilder laughed. "A woman after my own heart."

We started with raisin-studded pastries called fat rascals. "A Yorkshire specialty, my dear, you simply must try one," Mrs. Wilder said. Then we had scones with clotted cream and strawberry jam and finished with a Victoria sponge, a two-layer cake separated by a thin layer of raspberry jam. We washed it down with a pot of earl grey tea.

"That was delicious," I said when we had swallowed our last bite.

"Well, I'm glad you're seeing and tasting a bit of Yorkshire," said Mrs. Wilder.

"Mum divides this island in two," said Alec. "North Yorkshire and everywhere else. In fact, I'm pretty sure that's how she sees the known world."

"Cheeky!" But her eyes laughed.

That night, we watched *Coronation Street* on the small black-and-white television in the front room. Alec and I sat on the loveseat, his arm around my shoulder and Alice curled up on my lap. Mrs. Wilder sat in her chair, knitting.

"Alice likes you," she observed during a commercial for toothpaste. "Otherwise, she'd be all over my knitting."

The phone rang. Mrs. Wilder picked up the receiver. "Hello? One moment please."

She turned to Alec. "For you. A woman."

I sat up straighter, and Alice bolted off my lap. Why would a woman call Alec at his mum's house? Something—I wasn't sure what—gnawed at the back of my mind.

Frowning, Alec picked up the receiver. "Oh, hi, Mrs. Hall. Oh, Thursday. I'd forgotten. Yes, thanks for ringing. Bye." Heavily, he replaced the phone.

"What did Mrs. Hall want?" I asked. Whatever it was, he didn't look too happy about it.

"*Top of the Pops*," he replied sourly, sitting beside me on the sofa. "We're performing on Thursday to promote the new single. Dave, bless him, had a feeling I'd forgotten. He tried to call me at home, and when he couldn't reach me, he rang Mrs. Hall. So I'll have to drive you back to Manchester on Wednesday morning, not Thursday. I'm sorry."

I tried to hide my disappointment. "You have to do what you have to do," I said lightly. Over the last couple days, immersed in our private world, I'd almost forgotten how he made his living.

"And I'm sorry, Mum," said Alec. "I'd been hoping for a bit more of a visit."

"Well, we'll enjoy what we do have," said Mrs. Wilder. "Now I'm just wondering what to do about tea tomorrow."

"I'll get us something at the pub," replied Alec absently.

"No." Mrs. Wilder shook her head vigorously. "You see, I'd planned to have Peter, Jennie, and the kids round on Wednesday. I'd ask them for tomorrow, but I've got a meeting at church—"

"No need to worry, Mum. The three of us can grab something before or after your meeting."

"But you'll want to see your brother."

"As a matter of fact, I don't." A steely note, one I had not heard before, had crept into Alec's voice.

I held my breath. Perhaps it was inevitable a scene like this would ensue.

"He's your brother!" Mrs. Wilder sounded shocked.

"I think you'll find he feels much the same way. We've got nothing to say to each other, and it's best we see as little of each other as possible for everyone's sake. I'll thank you to remember it."

Mrs. Wilder's small face was flushed. When she spoke, her accent was thicker than ever. "And I'll thank you to remember that I'm your mother. Alec, I am not naïve though I've not traveled all around the world like you. I know there's summat between you and your brother, and I know it's Peter who's to blame. Mostly. I know what he said at your dad's funeral. But he wants to see you. When he heard you were coming home, he asked if he and Jennie could come round. I didn't have the heart to say no, and I hope you won't either."

Alec looked at the floor. "I didn't know," he mumbled.

"No, you didn't. Now, I'll ring Jennie and tell her about the change in plans." She reached for the phone.

Alec rose from the loveseat. "I'll ring, Mum," he said quietly.

"The number is—"

"I know it."

Mrs. Wilder's eyes met mine. Almost simultaneously, we rose from our seats and withdrew to the kitchen and sat opposite each other at the table. Mrs. Wilder folded her small hands and clucked. At the moment, she looked like a deflated sparrow.

"I'm so sorry you had to hear that row, Elsie—oh, I mean Miss Farrell."

"Please call me Elsie. And it's fine. Alec told me about what happened last summer."

Mrs. Wilder shook her head. "It's hard enough being an old widow before my time, but I don't like feeling that I've lost a son or that they've lost each other."

We sat in silence for a few minutes. Then Alec appeared. He sat beside me and placed an arm around my shoulder.

"Well?" said Mrs. Wilder.

"We're invited round for tea tomorrow," said Alec. "Half-past six. Jennie answered the phone. I suggested meeting at the pub, but Jennie was adamant we were to come to them."

"Well, that will be nice," I said. But my cheerfulness sounded brittle, even to me.

"I just hope Peter agrees with you," said Alec.

Eighteen

Tuesday passed pleasantly enough. Alec and I talked of going for a walk on the North York Moors, but the forecast mentioned rain. So we contented ourselves with a walk around the village capped by a lunch of cheese and tomato sandwiches at the pub. Every spot yielded an anecdote. There was the football pitch where, as a fifteen-year-old midfielder, Alec had distinguished himself in a match against a rival team. There was the Huntsman's Horn, the local pub where he and his friends had first gotten embarrassingly drunk the following year. He could remember buying penny candy at the shop when he was about four or five. And there was his dad's repair shop, of course.

We viewed it from a respectful distance on the opposite side of the street.

"It was more modest when Dad was at the helm," said Alec. "Dad didn't want to sell petrol, just repair cars. Peter was always at him to put in a pump. Now he's got his way." His tone was resigned, rather than bitter.

"Of course, the village could use a petrol station, really," he added.

I dressed carefully for the evening. If there was trouble between Alec and his brother, I didn't want to add to it. I wanted to look nice, but unobtrusively so as if I were out for a drink at the local or perhaps, round to Larry and Sally's for a bite. I wore a knee-length orange dress with white buttons and a peter pan collar and hoped I wouldn't be over or underdressed.

I wondered what Jennie would be like. Would she be determined to dislike me because of what lay between Peter and Alec?

I glanced at myself in the small mirror over what had once been Peter's desk. It struck me as amusing that I was even more nervous about a meal with an ordinary Yorkshire couple as I had been about meeting rock stars and their wives.

We discussed whether we should walk or drive to their house and settled on driving. "For the sake of the weather and your shoes," said Alec.

"What's Jennie like, then?" I asked in the car.

"The sort Peter would end up with, but nice enough," replied Alec.

I wanted to inquire further, but we had already reached our destination.

Peter and Jennie lived in a brick semidetached house in a new housing development just outside the village. A large burgundy sedan and a smaller green one that resembled a Volkswagen Beetle were parked in the driveway. Alec would know their make and model. I didn't.

"They have two cars," I said. Most families, British and American, were lucky to have one.

"It should keep them one step ahead of the neighbors."

Alec reached into the backseat and withdrew a bottle of wine he'd purchased at the shop earlier. He looked casual and yet polished in his brown corduroy sport coat, and I was proud of him as we walked to the front door, his arm around my shoulder.

As we approached, the door opened. They must have been watching for us. A man and woman stood in the doorway. Small faces peered at us from the front bay window. I waved, and instantly the faces vanished.

"Hello, Alec," said Peter. Everything about him was stiff, his posture, his voice, his short light brown hair, even the hand he extended to his brother.

"Pete." Alec spoke with a casualness I knew he must be feigning. "Good to see you, mate. Hello, Jennie." He kissed the woman's cheek.

"Nice to see you again, Alec," said Jennie. She wore a short-sleeved light green trouser suit. A few inches taller than I, she was slight with short, banged blond hair. I couldn't yet tell whether she was pretty.

"Pete and Jennie, meet my Elsie."

I couldn't help but be pleased to be described that way, so I was able to summon a real smile as I shook their hands. Jennie returned my smile rather nervously, and even Peter's features softened a bit as he looked into my face. He might have been good-looking if he relaxed.

"Well, come in, then," said Peter.

We stepped into the hall, and the two faces that had appeared at the window peered at us from around a corner.

"I see you," said Alec. He scooped the eldest, a blond boy of about five, into his arms and held him aloft.

"Tim's not keen on strangers," said Peter.

But the child laughed delightedly. "Hello, Uncle Alec," he said.

"Hello, Tim," said Alec, placing him on the ground.

Tim pointed at me. "Is that your American fancy woman?" he asked.

Peter grimaced, and Jennie flushed. "You mustn't say such things, Tim," she muttered.

I bit my lip to suppress my laughter. It was the first and probably the last time anyone would describe me that way. What reputation had I incurred in the Wilder household?

"Well, Miss Farrell is American, and I think she looks quite fancy," said Alec lightly. "In fact, I quite fancy her."

He turned to the younger child, a little blond girl of about three, who was clutching Jennie's trouser leg.

"Hello, sweetheart."

"She's just a bit shy today," said Jennie. "Say hello to Uncle Alec and Miss Farrell, Patty."

But Patty chewed on her collar and regarded us both with large blue eyes.

Peter coughed. "Come into the lounge," he said. "Have a drink before dinner."

"Thanks," I said, stepping toward the doorway.

"I meant Alec," he said stiffly.

I froze. I'd been in the house only two minutes. In that time, I'd been called a prostitute, and I'd misconstrued an invitation. Perhaps basic Yorkshire etiquette eluded me.

"Come into the kitchen, Elsie," said Jennie. She smiled uncertainly again, and I followed her into that room.

It was a modern kitchen—rather trendy, I supposed—with its avocado countertops and appliances. She stood in front of the stove, stirring a pot. I stood, hands folded, facing her back.

"Is there anything I can do?" I asked.

She darted a smile at me. "No. Make yourself at home."

I'd never felt less so.

I could hear the voices from the lounge.

"I see Mum's still got her old black-and-white telly," said Alec. "I've offered to buy her a color television, but she insists she prefers black-and-white. 'I've gotten used to seeing *Morecambe and Wise* a certain way,' she says. 'I wouldn't recognize Eric and Ernie in color.' It's quite sweet, really."

"Well, it's more about you than Mum, isn't it?" replied Peter.

"What do you mean?"

God, it was starting already.

"Oh, you want her to see you in all of your glory on *Top of the Pops*, and you want to be the great man buying things for Mum." Peter was bitter.

"A color TV's not much these days. Either of us could stand one." Alec's voice was surprisingly even.

"But it's not just the television, is it? You had to write a big check when the church roof needed repair. The *Reston Record* had an article: "*Top of the Pops* to the Top of the Steeple" or some such rubbish. And you hadn't darkened that church door since Dad's funeral."

"Are you one of the faithful, then?" Now Alec was scornful.

"We go now and then. Jennie sends Tim to Sunday school."

"How old are Tim and Patty?" I asked.

Eyes wide, Jennie turned. I realized she was as absorbed in the exchange next door as I was.

She smiled gratefully. "Five and three."

"They're adorable," I said. "Patty has such pretty eyes."

"Oh, thank you." She hesitated as if reaching for a question to ask me. "Where in the States are you from?"

"New Jersey."

"Jesus! I'm in your house five minutes, you hand me a whiskey, and next thing I know, you tell me everything that's wrong with me. I was right, Peter. You are a fucking prick."

"That language may work in your world, but it doesn't work in mine," Peter shouted. "I've got two kiddies in the front room and Jennie just in the kitchen."

"This is a lovely kitchen," I said brightly. "I like this shade of green."

I could hardly believe my ears. I didn't like the color at all.

"Thanks," replied Jennie. "I saw it in a magazine."

"If we're talking about women and children, how about Elsie?" Alec said. "How do you think she felt when she heard herself called a fancy woman though she was a good sport about it? And Timmy must have picked up that word somewhere, and it wasn't at Sunday school."

"Well, given your life and the women you've had, what were we to think? You can't have it both ways."

Alec sighed. "I won't ask you what you mean by that. Look, I came here tonight for Mum's sake and for Dad's. I know that's why you invited us. Can we make it work for them?"

There was a pause. "Yes," said Peter finally.

Dinner went surprisingly well. Tim and Patty were well-behaved and smiley, rather like children in an advertisement. Perhaps Jennie had gotten them from a magazine as well. Jennie asked me again where I was from in the States. Peter inquired politely what I was studying and if I liked Manchester. He had once eaten some bad fish and chips there. I asked Peter about how business was in Reston, and I asked Jennie where she grew up. Alec inquired about Jennie's parents and sister, and she asked him about the weather in Kent. We assured Jennie the chicken was delicious, and Peter admitted the wine was decent.

"He started it," I said when we were safely inside the Rolls. Somehow, I felt closer to Alec after this visit.

"Yes," said Alec. "But I shouldn't have mentioned Mum's telly. He's sensitive about the benevolent son bit."

"But it would have been anything," I said. "I mean, if you'd talked about the weather in London or mentioned something about the BBC studio, you'd have been showing off. You couldn't win."

"No, I couldn't. I can't. But I think things will be all right between Peter and me from now on."

I shot a glance at his profile. "After what just happened?"

"Oh, we'll never be mates. But we both know we've got to make it work once a year or so, if only for Mum's sake."

"I can see that."

"I did win in one respect, though."

"Oh?"

"I have you."

We were outside Mrs. Wilder's cottage. He parked the car and turned to me, his dark eyes smiling into mine.

Then he pulled me close to him and his mouth was on mine, and there was no one in the world but us.

It was a shame we were sleeping in separate rooms.

Nineteen

The next morning, I rose early, around six. I donned my dressing gown and wandered downstairs to make tea. Mrs. Wilder had encouraged me to do so whenever I wanted a cuppa.

Mrs. Wilder sat at the kitchen table. Atop the table My Lady regarded me with large round eyes as Mrs. Wilder stroked her forehead with one finger.

"Good morning, Elsie. Let me get you a cup of tea."

"I'm so glad you're an early riser, my dear," said Mrs. Wilder, setting a steaming cup before me a few minutes later. "I was hoping we could have a bit of a chat."

I inhaled the tea's aroma and added two heaping spoonfuls of sugar before wrapping my hands around the hot cup. "Thank you," I said, "for the tea and your kindness. You've made me very welcome, Mrs. Wilder."

"Call me Ruth. Well, you've been an easy guest, the easiest I could ask for. And while it's been lovely to have you for your own sake, I'm grateful that you've given my son back to me." Her brown eyes were very moist.

"But he was always yours," I faltered.

Mrs. Wilder nodded. "That he was. But he'd not been home in some time because of what lay between him and his brother. I know I've you to thank for his visit; Alec's admitted as much."

"I'm glad," I said simply. It was the truth, and I couldn't think of anything else to say.

"And I'm lucky, and so is Alec," Mrs. Wilder continued. "When I think of Sher—all the girls he might meet through his work—he's a very lucky man indeed. I expect we'll be seeing a lot more of each other."

"I hope so."

I drank some more tea, and Mrs. Wilder, or Ruth as I must learn to think of her, began talking about her cats. I had always been shy around boys' parents; even the prospect of meeting Jules's progenitors had turned my stomach, not that he'd ever mentioned introducing us. But I felt nearly as at ease around Ruth as I did my own mother.

I wondered how seriously to take the fact that Ruth expected to see more of me. Had Alec conveyed that he was serious about me? I hardly allowed myself to hope so.

After a full English breakfast, Alec and I left for Manchester. "I won't have you driving on an empty stomach," Ruth declared. The sun was shining, and the air was mild for late April, so we sped down the motorway with the windows open. He held my hand, and we laughed a great deal.

In a couple hours, we arrived in Manchester. But instead of stopping in front of Mrs. Barrymore's rowhouse, he parked the Rolls in front of the Midland. He turned off the engine and looked at me.

"This isn't Mrs. Barrymore's house," I said.

"It is not." His mouth was firm, but his eyes laughed.

"Just what are you planning?"

"Wouldn't you like to know?"

Two hours later, we reentered the Rolls.

"I wanted to say goodbye properly," said Alec. "And since we'd been sleeping in separate rooms for three nights, this seemed the place for it." His hand rested on my thigh as we drove away.

When we were parked opposite Mrs. Barrymore's house, Alec put his hands on my shoulders. His dark eyes smiled into mine.

"I love you, Elsie," he said. Then he kissed me.

"I—I love you too," I said when we were apart. My voice was trembling. No guy had declared his love for me since I was seventeen.

I recovered my composure. "Do you always declare your love to girls after you've taken shameless advantage of them?" I said lightly.

"In this instance, yes."

He walked me to Mrs. Barrymore's front door, where we kissed again. "I'll be tied up at the Beeb all day tomorrow, but I'll ring you on Friday," he said.

He pressed my hand, and then he was off in the Rolls.

Just a few days earlier, I'd suspected him of buying perfume for another woman. Then, on Easter, I'd even feared he might have abandoned me out of boredom. And now I had entered a fairy tale: the man I hadn't allowed myself to trust had declared his love for me.

Mrs. Barrymore welcomed me back with more warmth than I had anticipated.

"And how was the party with Mr. Wilder's musical friends, Miss Farrell?" she asked at dinner that evening.

She was impressed when she heard it had taken place at a Georgian manor house. To put her off from asking more questions, I briefly described our time with his mother in Yorkshire.

"What a privilege to see more of this beautiful island, especially in the company of Mr. Alec Wilder," said Ravi. "I hope I am able to visit Yorkshire and other interesting places during my time in this country."

"Your curiosity does you credit, Mr. Singh," said Mrs. Barrymore indulgently. "You be sure to make the most of your time here."

Lila hadn't yet returned from Bristol, and I missed being able to exchange glances with her.

I didn't go to uni the next day. The summer term hadn't begun, and in any case, the last third of the course wouldn't consist of lectures. There would be a few tutorials with Timothy Burgess, the Glaswegian lecturer supervising my dissertation, but I would be alone, for the most part, with my Royalist poets and their protectorate censors.

On Thursday morning, I reviewed some notes I'd taken before my holiday. The exercise was reassuring. Although I had my work cut out for me, I knew how I wanted to structure my dissertation, and I had completed almost all of the research.

In the early afternoon, my mom called. We'd only spoken briefly on Easter, so she wanted to hear all about my trip. She was interested in everything from the antics of Ruth's cats to the visit to Mount Grace Priory to the description of what we'd eaten at Betty's. It occurred to me that she and Ruth would get along very well. She was indignant when I told her about the dinner at Peter and Jennie's, especially the American fancy woman remark.

"That son of a bitch!" she cried. She rarely swore, especially in front of Nana, but when she was provoked, the epithet leapt to her tongue. "I don't know how you could stand there and be so nice to them."

"It was for Alec's sake and his mum's."

"I can see why you and Alec did your best," she said. "But I hope you don't have to see much of them. Peter sounds like Aster's pet horse, and that wife of his sounds useless."

"You know, I think they're all right," I said, "outside of the thing between Peter and Alec. Just dull."

I fidgeted with the phone cord.

"Alec said he loved me for the first time when we said goodbye yesterday," I said. "And his mum said she expected to see more of me. I'm not sure what it means."

"I do!" she exclaimed. "I'm so happy for you, honey."

Along with joy, there was relief in her voice. Like Maggie, she'd feared my rock star suitor was taking advantage of me although she'd done a better job of hiding her misgivings. I couldn't blame them. Incredulous that someone like Alec could really love me, I'd harbored the same suspicions.

In the late afternoon, Lila returned to Mrs. Barrymore's house.

"How was "Aunt Harriet?"" I asked in the corridor.

"Much the same as ever," replied Lila coolly. "Though her hair was a bit longer."

I suggested going out for a curry. So over plates of chicken tikka masala, we dissected our week away. She and Harry had attended a concert in Bristol, and they'd visited friends in Oxford. As always, she was interested in my doings. She was bemused by Cheryl's behavior at the party and indignant at my reception at Peter and Jennie's house. She smiled at my account of Ruth and her cats.

Afterward we repaired to The White Mouse. With the aid of a pint of lager, I confided both Ruth's assurance that she would see me again and Alec's declaration of love.

"Of course, I'm not sure how seriously I should take it," I said.

Her smile was indulgent. "I think you can take them both at face value. I would!"

When we arrived at the house, Mrs. Barrymore opened the door. She stood at her full height, gazing at us through her thick glasses.

"Good evening, Miss Hedges," she said coldly. "I suppose you have something to say for yourself, Miss Farrell."

Lila and I exchanged glances. It was only nine o'clock, an hour before our curfew. Perhaps I had left the tap on.

"What's wrong, Mrs. Barrymore?" I asked.

"What's wrong?" she expostulated. "It's the lies you've been telling. Mr. Wilder is no more a violinist with the Royal Philharmonic than I am the Queen Mum. I just saw him on *Top of the Pops* prancing about in leather pants and platform heels."

Twenty

I had forgotten that Mrs. Barrymore was a paid-up member of Mary Whitehouse's National Viewers' and Listeners' Association. Although she despised most of the popular music of the past fifteen years, she felt compelled to watch *Top of the Pops* periodically, a grim vigil that always corroborated her belief in the country's declining moral standards.

"What I feel worst about is Mr. Singh," said Mrs. Barrymore at breakfast the next morning. "He was so impressed with Mr. Wilder—the person he thought Mr. Wilder was anyway." She sniffed.

I avoided eye contact with Lila. Ralph's eyes were wide as he bit into his toast and marmalade. No doubt he was relieved his aunt had not accused him of being complicit in the deception—yet.

Ravi's smile encompassed everyone at the kitchen table.

"It is my fault, really," he said. "I confused Mr. Alec Wilder of Serval with Mr. Alec Wilde of the Royal Philharmonic. Mr. Wilder, though not a classical violinist, is a kind man. He allowed me to believe he was with the orchestra because he did not want to disappoint me. Miss Farrell, in addition to being a brilliant scholar, is also a kind young lady, and so she went along with this ruse. It was what you English call a little white lie."

Mrs. Barrymore's mouth softened into something that might have passed for a smile.

"I'd call it more than that, Mr. Singh, but your generosity does you credit," she said. "Now how about another slice of toast and marmalade?"

Lila's kohl-rimmed grey eyes laughed over her teacup. I beamed at Ravi, hoping that I showed enough teeth to convey gratitude, amusement, and the offer of a pint.

Ravi's slight nod, accompanied by a brilliant smile, suggested I had succeeded.

I spent some time in the university library that morning before repairing to the postgraduate office for a cup of tea. Clara and Larry had had the same idea, so we settled down for a cuppa and chat. Belle occupied a settee on the other end of the room. She waved airily at us, but declined my offer of tea.

Larry had had a quiet Easter though he and Sally had managed a few days with their families in Devon. Clara said hers had been duller still although she and Angie had gone to the cinema once.

"But I think your holiday was a little more exciting than ours," said Clara. "How was the party?"

"Less intimidating than I thought it would be. The band and crew were all really friendly, and I met the band's wives as well. They were lovely as well. And I met the opening act, a singer called Cheryl Wiles."

Larry and Clara nodded; they had heard of her.

Out of the corner of my eye, I saw Belle lean forward slightly. A little smile flickered over her lips as she set down her book and set about rolling a cigarette. She kept smiling as she lit her cigarette and sat back with one arm folded over her chest.

"Then we spent a few days with his mum in Yorkshire," I continued. "It was a spur-of-the-moment decision. She was lovely, very warm." I briefly described her work with Cats Protection and our outings to the priory and Betty's.

I could feel Belle's green eyes on me. Why was she so interested in our jaunt to Yorkshire? She seldom cared about what I had to say unless she decided to sneer at my interest in the seventeenth century.

"I met his brother and sister-in-law as well," I said as nonchalantly as possible. Of course, the less said about them, the better. "I'm just relieved we got on so well—you know, meeting the parents and such."

"I'm not surprised," said Larry. "Alec's lovely, so it makes sense his mum would be nice as well."

"Of course, she liked you, pet," said Clara. "You're the daughter-in-law parents want."

She looked troubled, and I realized she was no longer thinking solely of my romance.

"How long will Alec be on tour?" Larry asked.

"Just through the middle of June—about a month and a half. They'll play a few dates in Britain and then some on the continent and then back to Britain for a few gigs."

"How do you feel about Cheryl opening for Serval?" Belle asked from the sofa.

Was she on a first-name basis with pop stars? There was something grating about her familiarity.

"Well, most acts tour as a double bill," I said lightly.

Belle tittered. "Yes, but most musicians don't go on tour with their ex-girlfriends."

"What?"

Someone inhaled sharply. Clara, I supposed.

Belle blew smoke at the ceiling. "You didn't know Alec and Cheryl were an item? I assumed you did. It was common knowledge; all the magazines were full of gossip about them last year. The *Jackie* and *Popswop* editors had such fun with the titles: "Wilder about Wiles" and "She's Got her Wiles in Wilder." Not that I read them, of course. But my little sister does."

She laughed as she leaned forward to stub out her cigarette. She was finished with it and with me.

Twenty-One

"I wouldn't take it to heart, pet," said Clara. "Belle will say anything to get a reaction, especially from you."

We stood outside the library, our hands stuck deep in our pockets. The sky had become overcast; I wished I'd brought a jacket.

"She seemed very knowing," I said slowly.

"She always does, especially when she knows nothing. Look, Elsie, the next time you talk to your bloke, just ask him. It'll clear the air, and you'll know one way or the other. In any case, he took you to see his mum."

Clara was right, I reflected as I stared at a volume of seventeenth-century poetry in the library. Belle would say anything to get a rise out of me. I could kick myself for showing her how much her tidings bothered me. For God's sake, I should have emulated Belle by feigning knowledge of the relationship. "Of course, but that's history," I might have uttered. "Besides, Cheryl and I get on splendidly."

But I had never been a very convincing liar. I wasn't even very good at deceiving myself.

And Belle's revelation explained a lot.

There was the party at Mike's house: Cheryl's fixation on Alec and the challenging stares she had cast in my direction. No doubt that was why Mandy had whisked me away to the sideboard. Come to think of it, even Alec's bandmates had been kind in their way, trying to change the subject and thus take the focus off Cheryl, Alec, and me.

And Alec, I recalled, had not been present during Cheryl's grand entrance. He must have absented himself when she appeared, joining the crew on the other side of the room. He had rejoined me when he discovered me chatting alone with Mandy.

Had he feared a confrontation between his girlfriend and his ex-girlfriend?

It was probable that Cheryl was part of his past. But she was part of his present as well. They would be on tour together for a month and a half. They would be thrown together, and though she was difficult—tempestuous was the word that leapt to mind—she was very attractive.

As Belle had remarked, most musicians didn't go on tour with their ex-girlfriends.

Before me, lines about wanton blushes and loyalty to kings ran together. I closed the book.

At dinner that night, Ralph was more animated than usual. He'd been invited to dinner at Miss Adams's house.

"Apparently, her dad's quite keen to meet me," he said. "Her mum's making roast lamb."

"That's lovely, Ralph," replied Mrs. Barrymore. "I know you'll make an excellent impression on Mr. and Mrs. Adams. It's encouraging when nice young people get together."

She looked significantly at me before taking another mouthful of potatoes.

Lila's grey eyes met mine. While I would ordinarily have found Mrs. Barrymore's disapproval entertaining, I couldn't summon a smile. After all, I didn't know how much longer my not-nice young man would be mine or whether he was mine at all.

The phone rang in the front room. Mrs. Barrymore wiped her face ceremoniously with the napkin on her lap and rose from her seat. In most instances, she insisted on answering the phone herself. She also insisted on taking her time.

In a couple minutes, Mrs. Barrymore returned to the dining room. "A call for you, Miss Farrell," she said coldly.

"Hello," I said tentatively as I picked up the receiver.

"Hello, Elsie," said a northern voice.

I gulped. I had simultaneously yearned for and dreaded his call. Now I had no excuse but to talk to him.

"Hi, Alec," I said, then cringed. My voice was as small and young as it had been the first time he called.

He laughed. "Your little voice."

"How are you?" I asked in what I hoped was my normal tone.

"All right. We were at the BBC Studio for fourteen hours yesterday and then out late last night, so today's been lazy."

"There was some fallout from your appearance on the show," I said. Feeling more like myself, I told him about Mrs. Barrymore's epiphany. He laughed, especially at Ravi's attempt to cover for him.

"He's a good egg," said Alec. "I'll buy him a couple pints the next time I'm in Manchester. I suppose I'll have to be a bit more obsequious with Mrs. Barrymore as well. Speaking of which, we're playing in Sheffield in a couple weeks, and there's a few days between that show and our gig in Liverpool. I was thinking I could spend some time in Manchester with you."

If he were seeing Cheryl, would he take time out from the tour to see me?

"If that's all right with you?"

I must have hesitated a few seconds too long. "Yes, of course."

Perhaps my fears about Cheryl were unfounded. After all the tour hadn't started properly, they were playing their first show at the Rainbow Theatre the next day, and here he was already making plans to spend time with me.

"Lovely. Were you at uni today?"

"Yes, I did some work on my dissertation and had a chat with Cl—"

"Alec!" called a female voice. "We're going." There was something very imperious in her tone.

"I'm sorry, I've got to go," said Alec. "Here's Lucas, he wants to talk with you. I love you."

There was silence and then Lucas's voice.

"Hello, Elsie, my dear, is Lila available? Pam wants to take Lila up on her offer to look at the mummies, so perhaps we'll all see each other next weekend."

"Lucas and Pam are descending on Manchester on Saturday," said Lila when we chatted in the upstairs corridor later after dinner. "Apparently, the band's given him the weekend off, and Pam really does want to see the university's collection of mummies."

"It will be interesting to meet her," I replied.

I must have spoken with less enthusiasm than I had intended for Lila looked concerned. "Are you all right?" she asked cautiously.

"Mostly." I motioned her into my room.

Once we were both sitting on my bed, I told her, in a hushed voice, about Belle's revelation, the light it shed on Cheryl's conduct at the party, and my phone call with Alec that evening. Lila listened, her mouth tightening when I described Belle's triumphant air and Cheryl's behavior.

"Did you ask Alec?" she asked when I finished.

"No." The truth was that I was afraid of the truth.

"So at this point, you just have Belle's word for it. Hearsay."

"Yes. But she sounded convincing."

I hesitated a moment before continuing. "Have you heard any gossip about Alec and Cheryl?"

"Not that I remember. But I don't pay that much attention to that sort of thing. And even if it is true, it doesn't mean he feels the same way about her now. Especially if she's that unpleasant. And he did just take you to meet his mum."

She was always so sensible, this glamorous Cleopatra.

"Yes, but why go on tour with her if they're no longer together and she's such a nightmare?"

"Maybe they planned the tour before they broke up. It's probably quite hard to get out of arrangements like that."

"True. But he came when she called just now. I just made him sound like a dog. Not very flattering."

Lila smiled. "Maybe a group of them were going out. If it were me, I'd ask him. I'd have to know."

She was right, and maybe I would. Eventually.

"I think I'll research it," I said suddenly.

"How?"

"Belle mentioned a magazine called *Popswop*. Do you know where I could get back issues?"

"I should imagine the newsagent should have some," said Lila, laughing.

Somehow, I got through the weekend. My mom called Sunday morning while Mrs. Barrymore was still at church. Maggie's mother-in-law had been more unpleasant than usual, and Mom was indignant on Maggie's behalf. I was grateful for her ire; it made it easier for me to conceal my mood. Alec rang that afternoon, sounding tired, but cheerful. Mrs. Barrymore curtailed our conversation—"I'm expecting a call from my sister in Birmingham"—and for once, I was grateful for her interference, even when the Bromie sister didn't ring.

On Monday, before I went into uni, I stopped at the newsagent where I occasionally bought a copy of the *Guardian* or *Telegraph* or a Cadbury's Bournville chocolate bar. The proprietress seemed friendly, the sort who might have past issues of *Popswop* for me.

Her long face, framed by a greying permanent, beamed at me from behind the till. I placed a Cadbury's Bournville and the latest issue of *Popswop* on the counter.

"Thanks, my love," she said after I paid her.

I glanced around the shop. It was empty, apart from a man in a trenchcoat examining some magazines.

I leaned forward. "Do you have any back issues of *Popswop*?" I whispered.

The proprietress laughed, revealing a gap where her left incisor should have been.

"The way you asked, my love, I would have thought you were asking for rude pictures or tickets to a blue movie," she said loudly. "Who would have thought it of a well-spoken young lady like you? But there's naught to be ashamed of in wanting to look at a fine young man. David Cassidy, is it?"

My cheeks grew hot. "I'm at university!" Just how young did she think I was?

"I suppose he is a bit more for the younger girls," the proprietress continued. "Looks a bit like a girl himself, I've always thought. Not that I've an objection to long hair in the younger generation. That Brian from The Sweet or that Greg from Serval—now they're a reason to watch *Top of the Pops*. Just because we settle for something grey and paunchy doesn't mean we can't admire the young and fair. And if the husband watches for the girls in Pan's People, why then I can enjoy Brian and Greg prancing about in tight trousers. I wouldn't mind seeing their platform shoes under my bed."

How did she know I was looking for pictures of Serval? My cheeks must have been bright red by this point.

The reward for listening to this soliloquy was a wink accompanied by a stack of back issues of *Popswop*.

"We all can dream," said the proprietress with a knowing smile.

A singularly apt phrase, I thought when I sat outside Timothy Burgess' office later that morning. For, in a way, wasn't the idea that Alec Wilder could be seriously interested in me as ludicrous as the likelihood of a Brian or Greg dallying with the newsagent?

I'd arrived about three-quarters of an hour before my scheduled appointment, which left me with ample time to peruse my stack of *Popswop*. Most of the articles were short—in fact, the bulk of the publication seemed to be composed of photos—so it was relatively easy to skim and discard issues that contained nothing of interest. Why did the Osmonds and the Jackson 5 and Alice Cooper and Gary Glitter with his great staring eyes consume so much of so many issues? And there were features devoted to ephemera like stars' favorite lunches. Billy, Serval's bassist, was partial to egg and chips. I wondered how often Irene made them for him.

At last, in a November issue, I found what I was looking for in an article titled "Trials of Touring":

"'The hardest part is being apart from the one you love, really,'" said Serval's Alec Wilder. 'That's why Cheryl and I will tour together next spring,'

Apparently, the singer's "wiles" are too hard for Alec to resist."

Unrelated black and white photos of the stars mentioned accompanied the article. One showed Alec playing guitar on stage. He wore a metallic jacket, and the camera had captured him in full concentration, his parted lips revealing his crooked teeth. In her photo, Cheryl, clad in a pink dress with puffed sleeves, smiled softly at the camera. She looked yielding. Feminine, my mom would say.

Would anyone who'd loved her be able to look at me with a straight face?

"Miss Farrell?"

Timothy Burgess's round face, capped by disheveled white hair, gazed into mine. Behind his bottle glasses, his pale blue eyes frowned.

"Miss Farrell? I'm surprised at you. I had thought you were a young woman of some substance. In any case, I'm ready for your tutorial."

I opened my mouth and then remembered my mom's counsel about avoiding over explanations. "Better to say nothing than too much," she always said.

I bit my tongue and followed him meekly into the office.

Alec called every day that week. Since we only spoke for a few minutes, I managed to be cheerful enough. In fact, I was probably a bit more effervescent than usual, asking him questions about the tour and his gigs.

On Saturday, Lucas and Pam arrived in Manchester. Lila and Pam spent the afternoon looking at mummies—or corpses in sheets, as Lucas put it—and in the evening, we all convened at The White Mouse.

"Pam wants to see the authentic Manchester," said Lucas, grimacing at us over a pint of ale.

"I'm not sure The White Mouse is authentic Manchester," replied Lila. "It's a nice little pub, though."

Pam laughed. Plump and chestnut-haired, she was pretty in her long smock-style blue dress over a white turtleneck. There was something very bohemian about her.

"Oh, neither of us is the least bit interested in authenticity," she said. "I prefer irony in a pinch, and Lucas just wants a pint and an audience."

In a few moments, Lila and Pam were engrossed in a conversation about Pam's latest project, copper sculptures that would use the techniques of ancient Egyptian art to honor obscure dead artists. That left me alone, for all intents and purposes, with Lucas.

"How is being on tour?" I asked.

"All right," replied Lucas with an unlit cigarette in the corner of his mouth.

As he raised his lighter, I fired my next salvo.

"I mean, how is being on tour with Cheryl?"

Lucas unflicked his lighter and set it on the table before him. His bright dark eyes appraised me.

"Has Mandy been talking to you?"

"No, a girl on my course. And I read about it in *Popswop*."

Lucas lit his cigarette. "Well, I can't lie to you. Cheryl's difficult, a very difficult person."

"She and Alec used to be—"

"Yes. But that ended before Alec met you."

He didn't seem in the least concerned. In fact, he sounded bored.

"But why didn't he tell me?"

Lucas blew smoke out of the corner of his mouth. "Why? Because you're his girlfriend, that's why. He didn't want you to worry about anything, and there's nothing to worry about."

"Then why is she always summoning him?" I described the exchange I'd heard over the phone on Sunday.

Lucas shrugged. "She can't bear to be alone. That night, I think she made the guys in Serval eat with her since her back-up musicians had ducked out for a Chinese without her. That way, she can flatter herself that people—men—want to be around her. The crew will suffice in a pinch. She made do with Sean one night this week."

"But she's got a boyfriend, that nice tennis announcer," I said. "Surely he's enough for her."

Lucas laughed and threw an arm around my shoulder, squeezing me in a quick hug. "You're a sweetheart, you know that? Don't ever change."

From across the table, Pam smiled indulgently at me, while Lila's grey eyes regarded me with kind amusement. Just how old did they think I was?

"Thanks," I said sheepishly. "But Cheryl's very attractive. Men—Alec—could be drawn to her."

"Some people are drawn to housefires, but no one wants to be caught in one." He took another sip of his pint. "Now, Elsa, remember why you're here. You're in Manchester to earn an MA. Focus on your dissertation; the rest will take care of itself."

How old did he think I was? Thirteen? Perhaps I was regressing. In no time at all, I'd be snapping bubblegum and clipping photos of David Cassidy.

"You're very sagacious for your age."

Once again, Lucas laughed. " I can be a pompous twit. But never to worry, my dear. Alec knows the difference between you and Cheryl. For fuck's sake, he took you to see his mum."

I sipped my lager. Lucas was right, of course. But if some girls were for showing to Mum, weren't other girls for other things?

Twenty-Two

On Tuesday evening, Mandy called.

"Hello, love, I'm sorry it's taken me so long to ring," she said. "I've been after Dave to get your number from Alec, but he keeps forgetting, bless him. Anyway, I was wondering if you'd like to come down to London this weekend for a bit of shopping."

"That'd be lovely," I replied, "but I don't have a lot of spending money—"

"Oh, don't worry about money. I was thinking more of a browse. We'll have a look around the shops and then lunch. I could meet you at Euston, let's say half-eleven or noon?"

As I hung up the phone, it occurred to me that I might ask Mandy about Cheryl during our outing. She seemed more forthcoming than Lucas, and, as a woman, she would understand my feelings.

Lila raised her eyebrows when I told her about the outing over a pint at the King's Arms. "Lunch and shopping with a band member's wife? I'd say you have arrived."

"Fiancée and I'm not so sure I've arrived. In any case, I'm not sure what I should wear; after all, she'll be taking me to all sorts of fashionable London shops."

"I reckon she'll take you to the King's Road, maybe Biba. It should be quite cool, but you should be fine as you are."

"Have you ever been to either?"

"I went to Biba with some friends once, maybe twice during my first year or two of university. I think I bought a scarf. But for all the talk about spotting Twiggy or Mick Jagger, everyone goes to Biba. For the most part, it's not that expensive. There are girls who work in shops who buy clothes at Biba."

Hip London shop assistants with far greater knowledge of fashion than I. In a trendy boutique, I would be instantly identifiable as a nerdy, crass American.

Lila seemed to read my thoughts. "I expect a lot of people visit these shops hoping for a glimpse of celebrities. And in any event, you'll be with Mandy. She sounds really nice."

As always, Lila was reassuring. All the same, I dressed with care on Saturday morning, donning a short-sleeved yellow eyelet peasant blouse and a favorite pair of flares. I wasn't fashionable, but, at least, I could blend in as a fairly typical student.

"So you're going shopping in London," said Mrs. Barrymore ominously when she bid me adieu at the front door. "I hope you know what you're getting into."

I pondered this cryptic utterance after I boarded the train at Manchester Piccadilly. What could I possibly be getting into? Mandy and I would visit the shops, we would eat lunch, and then, in the late afternoon, I would take the train back to Manchester. Was Mrs. Barrymore worried that I might be embarking on a life of extravagance? She hadn't previously seemed as censorious of materialism as she had the other vices. After all, she had been more impressed with Alec's Mercedes than I was.

Somewhere between Stafford and Rugby, it occurred to me that she meant spending the day with a rock star's fiancée. In her mind, shopping in London, at least with someone like Mandy, was synonymous with all the excesses of the last decade. Step into the right—or wrong—shop, and you just might find yourself eating hash or taking part in an orgy, perhaps with the Rolling Stones.

It was nearly noon when the train pulled into Euston. Just outside the station, Mandy waited, looking stunning in a sleeveless turquoise jumpsuit with flared legs.

"There you are, love," she said, flashing her slightly gap-toothed smile. "So glad you could come. My car's just around the corner—piece of luck as it's unheard of to find a spot near Euston on a Saturday."

Mandy's car proved to be a purple Morris Mini. It suited her: lively and stylish, but somehow approachable.

"I thought we could start in the King's Road in Chelsea," she said as she started the car. "Then head to Biba in Kensington. Unless you're really hungry, then we could eat first. I'm fine either way; I love food."

"I'm fine. Mrs. Barrymore stuffed me with a full English breakfast, so I could wait a bit."

"Is that your landlady? She sounded very stern and disapproving when I rang."

"She is." Briefly, I described Ravi's efforts to persuade Mrs. Barrymore that Alec was in the Royal Philharmonic.

Mandy laughed merrily as she guided the Mini through London traffic.

"That is too funny! I'll have to tell Dave about that; he'll want to get Alec a violin or something, just as a prank. How do you do it? Boarding with someone like that, I mean?"

She was equally delighted with our efforts to elude Mrs. Barrymore's curfew and general disapproval.

"Aunt Harriet! I love it. If I meet Lisa, I'll be sure to ask her about her Aunt Harriet."

"Lila." But I knew Lila wouldn't mind.

When we arrived in the King's Road, I realized I had had nothing to worry about. It was warm for May, and the street teemed with pedestrians sporting all sorts of fashions, from long-haired, bearded types and their consorts in long dresses—hippies, my dad would call them—to young women in mini dresses and hot pants and high boots to people who looked as though they had dressed for the office, but somehow been borne into the crowd of shoppers on the street. I would blend in, and that was exactly what I wanted.

Mandy linked her arm in mine and kept up a running commentary about the shops we passed.

"There's Let It Rock, which sells mostly records and some clothing. The bloke who runs it wants to be different at all costs. And that shop there caters mostly to cross-dressers. That's where Serval and some other bands get their high-heeled boots." Again, she laughed. "Think of Alec and Dave shopping there."

We visited a dim shop, its air thick with incense. The interior consisted of tables draped with yellow and red silk and topped with statues of Buddha and various Hindu deities, including one with an elephant's head. I was a bit relieved when we escaped the incense and stepped back into the sunshine and bustle of the street.

"Excuse me, but what exactly did that shop sell?" I asked.

Mandy giggled. "You know, I'm not sure. Jewelry, I think, and perfume though it rather got lost amongst all the Buddhas. I don't really shop there myself, but I thought you might like to see it."

"The King's Road Experience."

"Exactly."

Next, we entered Citrus, a bright little boutique with orange walls and yellow curtains. The dresses were colorful, and they came in a variety of lengths. They weren't hung on racks like they were at Marks and Spencer or Dorothy Perkins or the stores I went to at home, but displayed at various places throughout the store. A wardrobe's door was open, revealing a rack of dresses; other items peaked behind other doors. A few items hung on hooks scattered around the store. Mandy selected a few items to try on, and she chose a few for me.

"You must try this on," she said of an orange miniskirt. "And this blue would be ravishing with your eyes."

The dress was just past the knee, and it consisted of the floatiest, most diaphanous fabric I had ever seen.

"It's beautiful," I admitted. "I'll try it on."

"You should get Alec to take you shopping."

"I never thought of it."

Mandy's smile widened. "You're sweet," she said. "No wonder Alec's mad about you."

In the changing room, once I donned the blue frock, I could hardly believe what I saw in the mirror. Even though changing clothes had made my curly hair frizzier, even though my makeup needed a touch up, the dress had transformed me. I was no longer mousy, sallow little Elsie, but someone glamorous with dark blue eyes and what the English called brown skin and what we called olive in New Jersey. The floaty fabric hugged my frame softly, so I appeared both slender and curvaceous.

Rather self-consciously, I stepped out of the changing rom.

Mandy's face broke into a smile. She was really very lovely.

"Wait until Alec sees you in that!" she exclaimed.

I felt the pressure of other eyes. A tall man in dark glasses gazed pointedly at me.

"Thanks," I said. "But he won't see me in it. It's a bit expensive."

"Well, I'll just pay for this skirt then, and we'll be on our way."

Once we were in the street, Mandy sighed. "I'm sorry, Elsie, but I think I'll get those sandals after all. I'll be just a minute."

A few minutes later, she reemerged, looking particularly cheerful.

"Let's see what's at Biba," she said. "Or maybe who's at Biba. Lots of people come on the off chance that they might see David Bowie or Mick Jagger."

"Have you ever seen them?"

Mandy shook her head. "No. Though Alec's probably told you the story about Bowie speaking to Dave in the BBC Studio."

"The time Bowie bumped into him in the makeup room?"

"Yes. Dave was going out, Bowie was going in, and he bumped Dave's elbow. He smiled and said, 'Sorry.' Dave never tires of telling that story!"

Biba proved to be a boutique in the Kensington High Street. With the plants on the store's periphery and the burgundy fabric draped over tables and chairs, it appeared to be a combination of a conservatory and a boudoir. The slender, fair-haired shop assistants were fashionably, but casually dressed. A clerk who couldn't have been older than seventeen wore denim overalls.

The clothes, I noticed, were less expensive than those in the King's Road boutique. At Mandy's insistence, I tried on a long yellow dress and a shimmery silver mini dress, but since I didn't like either of them nearly as much as the blue dress, it was easy to say no. After trying on something I loved, I didn't want to waste money on something mediocre, even if it was within my budget.

"Well, at least you've seen Biba," said Mandy when we once again found ourselves on the busy High Street. "Come back in the autumn; a Biba department store opens in September. There'll be a café and a food hall and all sorts of things."

"My course will be done by then, unfortunately," I said. "I'll be back in the States."

"Then come back for the Biba opening if nothing else," said Mandy lightly. "Now, where would you like to go for lunch? There's a lovely little trattoria just around the corner if you're in the mood for Italian food, and there's Cranks. It's a vegetarian restaurant with really nice nut roasts and salads though I'm not quite ready to give up my steak and kidney pud." She paused. "Or we could get afternoon tea at Harrods."

My eyes must have lit up because she laughed. "I thought you might like it, being new to London."

"When I was a little girl, I always wanted to have afternoon tea at Harrods," said Mandy once we were inside her Mini. "It sounded so posh. But my mum couldn't afford it. But when I was on my own, I was determined to go. I remember I was sharing a flat with a few girls in Croydon. I was seventeen, and I'd barely qualified as a hairdresser. So my friend and I took the bus to Knightsbridge and treated ourselves to afternoon tea. The waiters were a bit sniffy—we were so young, and we didn't have the accent they were used to. But that's all changed now. Except the accent, of course; that's still there."

"Of course, we're not smart enough for the Georgian," Mandy continued. "We'll come back in hats for that sometime. But we can get a lovely tea at the Dress Circle."

The Dress Circle proved to be a small, self-service café on the store's first floor. My eyes must have widened at the array of cakes, some of them topped with fruit and elaborate swirls of icing.

"It's hard to choose, isn't it, love? I can never decide on just one cake, so I always order two different ones."

We took our seats at small round tables flanked by short, round chairs. Over tiny sandwiches, piece of chocolate cake, and slices of Victoria sponge, we chatted. I learned that Mandy was twenty-two, a year younger than I was. Even though she lived with Dave, Mandy still worked as a hairdresser at a unisex salon in Chelsea a few days a week.

"Dave doesn't want me to work," she said. "But I enjoy the customers, and I like being busy. Half the time, I think he's nervous I'll run off with a customer—that's how I met him a year and a half ago. I cut his hair!"

"Of course, I'll stop once we get married," Mandy continued. "It'll be boring being home alone, especially when he's away, but that'll change once we have kids."

I swallowed a mouthful of Victoria sponge.

"It's funny," I said slowly. "I'm obviously at university because I want to teach, and I do like what I'm studying. But I think I wouldn't mind being at home. All that extra time for reading and writing."

"It would suit you, you being so bookish. Alec likes reading, too; you'll probably be very cozy with your books."

Why did she assume Alec and I were on the cusp of marriage and a comfortable old age in his library? She had some funny ideas. Then again, as Dave's fiancée, perhaps she would have some insights about Alec and Cheryl, ones that Lucas would lack.

It was time to ask.

"Mandy," I said, "how long were Alec and Cheryl together?"

Halfway through lighting a cigarette, Mandy froze.

Recovering her composure, she removed the cigarette from her mouth. "Who told you about that?"

I described the little scene in the postgraduate office.

"The stupid cow! But you've got nothing to worry about."

Like Lucas, she sounded assured. In fact, she seemed more annoyed with Belle than anything.

"But how long were they together?"

Mandy lit her cigarette. "I don't know. Ten months, maybe a year. The way Dave talks, Alec wasn't very happy during that time. I expect he's relieved to be rid of her."

"But they're together all the time, and she's so attractive." I told her about overhearing Cheryl summon Alec.

"Oh, Cheryl always just wants attention. She's like that with all men. I don't think anyone in the band or crew really likes her. Dave can't stand her!" Mandy waved her hand dismissively as if Cheryl's attractions were a puff of smoke.

"And Alec isn't the type to cheat, not when he's in love with someone like he is you. I feel really bad for Betty and Irene."

I was going to hear something interesting. To fortify myself, I downed the last of my tea.

"From the way Dave talks, Greg and Billy will go off with anything female when they're on tour," Mandy continued. "Greg and Betty used to row about it all the time, but now I think she's decided she's happy with her Mercedes. And besides, they've got a child, a little boy. To me, it's even sadder that she doesn't confront him about it anymore. And underneath it, I think she still loves him."

Although there was nothing reassuring about this conversation, I wanted to hear more. "And Irene?"

Mandy flicked ash from her cigarette. "She loves Billy. And she doesn't confront him. She just drinks a bit much when she's alone.

And takes sleeping pills. Though I hope that's passed now that she's going to have a baby—did you know she was expecting? I think they've only just started telling people about it, so it's quite early days yet."

I stared at my cup and saucer. At the party, I hadn't formed any impression about the women's marriages, not that I'd had much of a chance to observe them with their husbands. Like a child, I'd cared only about was how they'd treated me. They'd been welcoming, and so I was satisfied.

Now that I thought of it, there had been something fragile about Irene, a sadness beneath her slender prettiness.

"Do you see much of them?" I asked.

"Just here and there. We're not best mates, but they're nice girls. I'm just glad I've got Dave. And you've got Alec." She smiled her childlike gap-toothed smile.

"Now that we're here, we might as well have a look around," she said when we'd finished our tea. "The pet department is always fun—you'll never know what you'll see!"

In addition to poodle puppies and Persian kittens, the pet department boasted a baby giraffe and a zebra. Behind their glass partition, they looked like big stuffed toys, chewing their feed and surveying their surroundings with large, soft eyes.

"They're adorable," I said, "but it's so strange to see them in a store. In London."

"I know! A few years ago, two Australian blokes bought a lion cub here. They had him in their flat and they brought him to the furniture shop where they worked. They ended up bringing him to Africa when he grew up, I think. But you can order any sort of animal you like at Harrod's—even a baby elephant!"

After we admired luggage and chocolates and lingerie, Mandy drove me back to Euston Station.

"It's been lovely, Elsie," she said. "Let's do this again soon. Oh, and here's a little something for you." She reached into the backseat and produced a shopping bag. From it, she withdrew a smaller bag and handed it to me.

Mystified, I opened the bag. Soft royal blue chiffon billowed up at me.

"The dress! You shouldn't have!"

"Well, it suited you so much it would have been ridiculous not to buy it."

"Thank you!" Impulsively, I hugged her. It was hard to believe I'd ever been intimidated by the prospect of meeting her.

"You're very welcome, love. I just want to be there when Alec sees you in it."

She was so good at flattery. No wonder she was a hairdresser at one of the trendiest salons in Chelsea: she could make someone as unremarkable as me feel beautiful.

I thanked her again for the tea and the outing and exited the car.

"Oh, Elsie?"

I paused before the driver's side window. "Yes?"

For once, Mandy's brown eyes were serious. "You and Alec have something really special. Don't let two nasty cows ruin it."

Twenty-Three

Over the next few days, I replayed my conversation with Mandy. For the most part, I was reassured. After all, Alec called every day or nearly every day. And while we never talked for very long—it was Mrs. Barrymore's phone, after all—he was always attentive.

"That sounds like Mandy," he said when I told him about how she had given me the dress. "Let's have a proper evening out when I'm in Manchester so that I can see you in it. And when the tour is over, I'll take you shopping in London. Or Paris if you like. We could fly over, have dinner, and stay overnight, maybe make a few days of it and take in the museums."

And he always told me he loved me before he rang off.

When I felt optimistic, I remembered statements like these.

When my confidence waned, I recalled Cheryl's voice: "Come on, Alec, we're going." For it hadn't been just that time. On a few occasions, he'd hung up directly after her voice, sometimes shouty, always peremptory, summoned him.

"Some of us are grabbing dinner," he'd say. Or "The band and the crew are going for a drink."

After these exchanges, I reminded myself of what Lucas and Mandy had said about Cheryl's constant need for attention. But somehow, I kept thinking of Betty and Irene: Betty alone in her big house with only her little boy and her Mercedes for company and Irene clutching a drink and perhaps a jar of pills in front of the television.

Then I remembered how soft and alluring Cheryl appeared in the *Popswop* photo.

I tried to distract myself with work, and my dissertation made that easy. And since I ate two meals a day with Mrs. Barrymore and my fellow lodgers, I was never alone with my own thoughts for very long.

The following Friday, Alec was especially affectionate during his evening call.

"I have to wait three whole days to see you, Elsie," he said. "We'll do the show in Sheffield on Sunday, and then I'll be in Manchester by Monday afternoon. I won't have to leave for Liverpool until Wednesday morning, so we'll have two nights together."

When we hung up, it occurred to me that I might surprise him by appearing in Sheffield. I'd take the train, check into a bed-and-breakfast, attend the concert, and then present myself backstage. He'd be delighted, we'd repair to his hotel, and in the morning, we'd return to Manchester together.

And so I called the tourist information office, booked a room at a bed-and-breakfast, and bought a ticket to Sheffield.

Lila was quiet when I confided this plan to her on Saturday evening. The two of us sat on my bed, cups of tea in our hand. In her jade green satin dressing gown, she looked more unconsciously gorgeous than ever with her pale skin and gleaming black hair.

"But you'll be seeing him on Monday," she said.

Put that way, it did sound silly.

"Yes," I replied. "But this way, we get to see each other sooner. And I can surprise him."

"I think I surprised Harry once," remarked Lila. "I baked muffins."

My mother was more direct when we spoke on the phone the next morning. When I told her my plans, she said nothing.

Perhaps the line had gone dead. "Mom, are you there?"

"Oh, I'm here all right. Elsie, you know, you're a bright girl. A grown woman. I don't like to tell you what to do. But are you chasing this man?"

Blood rushed to my cheeks. "Mom, he wants to see me. He's coming to Manchester tomorrow."

"Then why are you going to see him?"

I opened my mouth, but found I could not answer.

Mom sighed. "Elsie, you're on your own in another country. You've done things I've never dreamed of doing, and God knows, you understand all sorts of things I don't. But I was fifteen when I met your father, and I always knew one thing: I was the prize."

When we said goodbye, I replaced the receiver slowly. She had a point. But I'd already booked my room and bought my ticket, and it surely wouldn't hurt to surprise Alec just this once.

And so that afternoon, I boarded the train to Sheffield. I checked into my room at a bed and breakfast a stone's throw from Sheffield City Hall, where Serval was performing. The proprietress was nearly as disapproving as Mrs. Barrymore when she heard I was in town to see Serval. I had a takeaway curry and then bought a ticket to the concert.

As I filed into the concert hall, I remembered the concert Lila and I had attended back in January. How astonished we had been when Sean, the humongous Irishman, had summoned us to the limo that transported us to the afterparty at the Piccadilly. Now I would be admitted backstage as Alec's acknowledged girlfriend.

I took my seat near the back of the hall.

"Hey, sweetheart, all alone tonight?"

A leering, pockmarked face topped by lank brown hair hovered close to mine. Beneath his denim jacket, he was skinny, but there was something menacing about the smile.

"Get lost!" I shouted.

"Oh, it's got claws," he sneered. But he left me alone after that.

I might be the guitarist's girlfriend, but to this guy, I was merely an unaccompanied bird. Thank God, shouting came naturally to me, at least in situations like these. Growing up in Jersey City was sometimes an advantage.

Cheryl opened. She looked lovely in a long green dress and high-heeled sandals, and I had to admit she was good. During the livelier numbers, she danced a bit, sometimes twirling a tambourine. But she closed her set with a poignant song, one I recognized from an earlier era. Her face changed. She was no longer the sparkling songstress or the imperious diva, but a wistful little girl.

Even Mr. Pockmark shouted and applauded heartily.

Then the girls emitted their wolf howls, and Serval came on stage. I realized, even more than I had the first time, how talented they were. Greg's voice switched easily from harsh to tender, Dave's arms soared over the drum kit, and Billy, whatever his relationship might be with Irene, could play bass.

And Alec could play guitar. Just a little.

After the encore, Mr. Pockmark tried again. "What's on tonight then, darling?"

I didn't answer, but made my way through the throng of concert-goers to the stage door.

Sean stood in front of the door, his arms crossed across his chest. Perhaps he thought it made him look more imposing.

At first, he frowned at my approach.

"No more girls backstage, sweetheart—oh, Miss Farrell, I'm sorry. I didn't recognize you. Alec's at the back—think I saw him in front of the dressing room just now."

He opened the door. It wasn't surprising he hadn't recognized me. In my jeans, I was virtually indistinguishable from most of the other girls at the concert.

I found myself in a corridor that, though it was illuminated by garish bulbs, seemed dim. It was the sort of light that could bring on a headache.

Off the corridor were open doors. I peeked into the first one. The band's techs were sorting equipment. In the room's far corner, a man and woman stood. The man's back was toward me, but I could see the girl. Blond and slight, she sported a white crocheted minidress that ended just below her rear. As Mrs. Barrymore would remark, it covered so little it was hardly worth wearing.

She was very animated; in fact, she was smiling up at the man. I couldn't hear their conversation, but I heard her giggle and then a baritone chuckle.

Then the man leaned forward and put an arm around the girl's waist. His hand rested casually on her behind. His head turned slightly, enough to reveal his profile with his drooping mustache.

There was the pungent smell of tobacco.

"He loves his fiancée; he really does," said a grim voice at my elbow.

Lucas stood beside me in a rumpled undershirt, a hand-rolled cigarette resting in the corner of his mouth.

Dave pulled the girl closer to him and smiled lazily down at her. I couldn't look anymore.

"She's not as pretty as Mandy," I said indignantly.

"No, she's not," replied Lucas in the same grim tone.

"Then why do they do it?" My voice was shrill, unlike itself.

Lucas shrugged and took a drag of his cigarette. "They're pathetic little tarts. She'll be able to tell her mates she shagged the drummer from Serval."

"No, I mean Dave."

"He's a fucking twit. He doesn't love that girl—if they talked for ten minutes, he probably wouldn't even like her—but he's got to find someone for tonight, and she'll do."

He took another drag. "They're all like that, really. Lovely blokes, but I feel bad for their wives."

"What about Alec?" I cried.

"I was leaving him out of it, my dear. Nice to see you by the way. I didn't know you were coming. Does Alec?"

"No, it's a surprise for him. Where is he?"

"Think he was in front of the band's dressing room just now—at the end of the corridor. Give us a bit to take this down, and let's grab a drink together, the three of us."

I headed down the hall. Something about the long corridor with its bright lights and dark corners unnerved me. Out of nowhere, a corner appeared. I felt as though I were in a labyrinth.

Perhaps some monster awaited me in this maze. I shoved aside the ridiculous thought.

Tentatively, I peered around the corner.

Alec stood in front of a door, his back to me and his arms folded across his chest. I opened my mouth to call him.

Cheryl stood before him, gazing up at him. Her face wore the same wistful expression it had during the encore, and her green eyes were luminous.

Even in the harsh light, she looked lovely.

She uttered something I couldn't hear and placed her hands on Alec's shoulders.

I didn't see any more. I couldn't.

I fled back down the hallway, nearly colliding with a guy carrying pieces of Dave's drumkit.

"Hey, watch it!" he yelled.

He was stocky with shoulder-length curly hair. I didn't recognize him from Mike's party. He was weird and unfamiliar like everything in Sheffield.

Near the exit, Lucas toted an amplifier. He started at my approach.

"Elsie! What's wrong? Where are you going?" he cried.

"Where I belong," I said.

One push of the door, and I was gasping in the night air that had suddenly become cold and inhospitable.

Twenty-Four

Somehow, I had enough presence of mind to hail a cab. Although the bed-and-breakfast was only a short walk from City Hall, I was dimly aware that Mr. Pockmark or someone far worse might be afoot.

The bed was narrow and the mattress hard, and I found myself twisting and turning. Still, in my present state, the softest cushions would not have soothed me.

Images of the evening and the previous few months played over and over in my brain. Mandy and Dave bantering at Mike's party. Mandy assuring me that Alec and Dave were not like their bandmates who would "go off with anything female." Dave with his arm around the girl in the crocheted dress. And Lucas's words echoed: "Lovely blokes, but I feel bad for their wives."

Cheryl's green eyes challenging me in Mike's drawing room as she said, "Well, if anything happens to my guitarist, I fully expect Alec to step in." Alec absenting himself from the group, and Mandy steering me toward the sideboard. Mrs. Wilder saying, "When I think of

Cher—all the girls he might meet through his work—he's a very lucky man indeed." Lucas and then Mandy asserting that the band and crew barely tolerated Cheryl.

And Alec and Cheryl on the cusp of an embrace in a dim corridor.

Near morning, I lapsed into a fitful sleep. But even then there was no relief. In my dream, Mrs. Barrymore sat at her dining room table, nodding her grey head sagaciously. "What did you expect?" she asked. "He's not a nice young man. You ought to have listened to Mrs. Whitehouse; she was clear about him from the beginning."

Then, my sister Maggie appeared. Her large light blue eyes were filled with tears, and she shook her head.

This was her way of saying, "I told you so."

Suddenly, my mom was there, her green eyes sorrowful and sympathetic.

"Oh, for God's sake, honey," she expostulated. "All you had to do was wait until Monday."

I woke with a start. It was Monday, it was seven o'clock, and in an hour, the landlady would be serving breakfast. I rose and dressed.

The bed-and-breakfast's proprietress, Mrs. Watkins, advertised a full English breakfast, and, in a purely technical sense, she delivered one. Certainly, the fried eggs, sausage, bacon, fried tomato, baked beans, mushrooms, and buttered toast were present. But the bacon had been fried beyond recognition, the tomato was runny, and the toast was nearly burnt. I declined the sausages as politely as I could. Although I normally had a hearty appetite for a small woman, I picked at the repast.

Mrs. Watkins, a thin woman with an iron grey permanent, sniffed derisively.

"Cooking's not to your taste, miss?" she asked.

"No, it's lovely," I replied dully. "My appetite's a bit off today."

"Hardly surprising with the hours you keep," she mumbled as I rose from my chair.

On the train back to Manchester, I realized what I had to do. I'd wrestled with the decision as I'd tossed and turned during the night, but now I knew the words I needed to say.

When I returned home, Mrs. Barrymore opened the door.

"Good morning, Miss Farrell," she said, her mouth drawn up tightly. "I trust you enjoyed visiting your friends in Sheffield."

"Yes, thank you," I mumbled.

"Two gentlemen rang late last night asking for you." There was no mistaking the sarcasm in her voice when she pronounced "gentlemen." "Mr. Wilder and someone called Lucas."

"Did—did they leave a number?"

"No, they did not." Mrs. Barrymore clearly considered herself benevolent for even relaying the message.

Upstairs, I went to knock on Lila's door. When there was no answer, I at first assumed she had gone to university. Then I remembered that she had left for Bristol that morning to attend a series of Egyptology lectures at Bristol University and to spend a few days with Harry.

She would never say, "I told you so."

I should have gone to university, but I didn't. I couldn't run the risk of running into even Larry and Clara and fielding their friendly inquiries, let alone seeing Belle and Jules. So I remained in my room and attempted to focus on Royalist poets during the protectorate. Those who survived had, for the most part, kept quiet, which is all I wanted to do for the foreseeable future.

In the midafternoon, the phone rang in the front room. My shoulders tensed as though I were bracing for a blow.

My fears were confirmed when I heard Mrs. Barrymore's heavy footfall followed by a knock on my door.

"Telephone for you, Miss Farrell," she said. Her disapproval was palpable.

Slowly, I descended the stairs and entered Mrs. Barrymore's front room, closing the door behind me. Even I deserved privacy during the conversation I was about to have.

"Hello," I said in the same small voice he had heard the first time he called me.

"Elsie, sweetheart, what's wrong?" Alec asked. "Lucas said you were backstage looking for me last night, and the next thing he knew, you were racing out the backdoor."

It was hard to believe he'd been embracing Cheryl during my flight; his voice was all tender concern.

I was silent. I was not prepared to confront him about what I'd seen the previous evening.

"Did something frighten you? Or someone? We've got a couple new guys in the crew, and I don't know them all that well. Did anyone bother you?" His tone was solicitous, but behind the gentleness, there was a readiness to deal with whomever it was, forcibly if necessary.

"No." My voice was smaller than ever.

"Did you see something that upset you?"

He must have taken my silence for an assent, for he sighed. "Lucas mentioned you'd caught a glimpse of Dave with another woman. Elsie, I know it must have shocked you, but Dave loves Mandy. That girl meant nothing to him at all."

This was supposed to reassure me? Next thing, he would be telling me that Cheryl meant nothing to him, and I was not to worry.

"Anyhow, don't say anything about it to Mandy," Alec continued. "It would devastate her, and Dave would be cut up if she broke it off."

"Of course not," I snapped. How old did he think I was? Ten? Then again, I had spent part of the night deciding what to do about what I had seen.

"I didn't think you would, really. Anyhow, I rang last night, but you weren't here."

"No, I was in Sheffield." My voice was dull.

"Of course." Alec chuckled, almost nervously. "I suppose I just wanted to speak to you after that. Anyhow, I'm in Manchester at the Midland. What do you say to dinner at Isola Bella tonight?"

He had spent the previous night—and God knew how many others—with his ex-girlfriend, he had just finished telling me his bandmate's infidelity meant nothing, and now we were supposed to carry on with our plans as if nothing had happened.

"No, thank you." My voice had become stronger, more resolute.

"Would you prefer The French?"

"No."

"A curry or a Chinese?"

"No, I mean I don't want to go to dinner with you. Anywhere."

Now, there was silence on his end of the line.

"What's the matter, Elsie?" asked Alec finally. He sounded bewildered and oddly young.

Now that I was on firmer ground, I could recite with confidence the speech I had prepared.

"Alec, I've enjoyed our time together," I said. "But we're from different worlds, and I suspect it's best we not see each other anymore."

I sounded like a prim little girl parroting dialogue from a soap opera or perhaps a paperback novel.

Alec was silent for a minute. "It's that blond bloke, isn't it?" he said finally. There was an ugliness in his voice, something I'd not heard before.

"Who?" What blond guy? Surely not Greg.

"Julian—whatever the fuck his name is. The one with the little ginger tart at the symposium. I don't fit in with your university friends, but he does. And he's got a plummy accent—I expect that weighs with an American."

"None of my university friends can stand Jules!" I cried. "They never could."

"But you can. Oh, I saw him looking at you that day though he was with that simpering idiot. And you had to ask me what I thought of them after the symposium. Oh, a rock musician was a nice trophy, but you had your heart set on him."

Was he really jealous of Jules? Part of me wanted to reassure him that he meant far more to me than Jules ever had. Then I remembered him and Cheryl in the corridor at City Hall, her hands on his shoulders.

"Alec! This has nothing to do with Jules," I said. "You fit into my world perfectly. It's I who don't belong in yours."

I took a deep breath.

"I wish you all the best, Alec," I said. "Goodbye."

I replaced the receiver and exited the front room.

I half expected to see Mrs. Barrymore lurking in the hallway, but Ravi hovered outside the door.

"Is everything all right, Elsie?" he asked. "I wished to make a call, but Mrs. Barrymore informed me that the line was engaged. I assure you I was not eavesdropping."

I nodded and chose to believe him. And if he had been listening at the door, what of it? The whole house would find out soon enough.

The phone rang again, and I jumped.

"Is that for you?" asked Ravi.

"Probably."

"Should I answer it?"

"Please don't."

His dark eyes were large and sympathetic. To show my gratitude, I tried to lift the corners of my mouth into a smile. When that failed, I raced up the stairs as if to escape the phone, which continued to ring, each peal shriller and more insistent than the last.

Twenty-Five

Everyone was extra kind at dinner that evening, so I surmised that Ravi must have told Ralph and Mrs. Barrymore about my disappointment. Ralph asked how my dissertation was going, and even Mrs. Barrymore made an effort.

"You must come to the church's jumble sale next weekend," she said, smiling. "It's always a bit of fun."

Cat figurines and used cardigans were antidotes for heartbreak. Flattering myself that I concealed my amusement, I thanked her. She really did mean well.

For the next couple days, I lay low. I thought of calling my mom or Maggie collect, but decided against it. I wasn't ready to talk to anyone about it. Once I put it into words, Alec would really be gone. So I stayed in my room, pouring over my books.

On Wednesday afternoon, the phone rang. At my desk, my shoulders tensed. Surely, he wouldn't try again? It was too much to hope.

Mrs. Barrymore's pumps sounded up the stairs and into the hallway. Then there was her rap, authoritative, even peremptory, at the door.

"Telephone call for you, Miss Farrell." Her accents were so disapproving, I hardly dared hope.

I almost flew down the stairs and into the front room.

"Hello!" I said breathlessly when I picked up the receiver.

"Hello, Elsie." But the voice that returned my greeting was not northern.

"Hi, Lucas," I said. I hoped my disappointment was not audible.

"Elsie, Alec said you've broken it off. What happened?"

"I don't belong in his world." Once again, I was young and prim, a little girl reciting the lines she had memorized.

"Elsie, is this about Mandy and Dave? Because if it is, it's got nothing to do with you and Alec."

I sighed. "It's not just that. It's Cheryl and Alec."

"I told you: that ended before he met you. You're the one he cares about."

"That night—Sunday—I saw them embracing."

"Where?"

"In the corridor of City Hall. In front of the dressing room."

"Are you sure that's what you saw?"

I opened my mouth. What had I seen exactly?

"Well, they were standing in front of the dressing room door," I replied slowly. "Cheryl was looking up at Alec and then she put her hands on his shoulders—"

"And then?"

"I don't know. That's when I bolted."

"And two minutes later, I found Alec and asked him what had set you running," said Lucas. "He had no idea that you'd been there or that you were even in Sheffield. And Cheryl was nowhere to be found. If that was an amorous embrace, it's most fleeting I've ever heard of."

"Maybe it was just a quick hug," I said. "Perhaps they're being discreet in front of the band and the crew."

"Discreet? You don't know Cheryl. Elsie, I think you witnessed Cheryl making an attempt on Alec. That's all."

I froze. Had I really ended things with Alec because I had misconstrued a scene?

"But she's so attractive," I said feebly.

"So appealing her own band can't stand her," countered Lucas roughly.

"Look, Elsie, I have to set up for tonight's show," he continued. "We're in Liverpool tonight, and then we're in Dublin for the next two nights. I'll give you the telephone numbers of the hotels where Alec will be staying here and in Dublin."

Numbly, I scribbled them on the back of one of Mrs. Barrymore's church newsletters, the nearest scrap of paper I could find.

"You couldn't talk to Alec for me?" I asked.

Lucas emitted something halfway between a snort and a sigh.

"Elsa, my dear, I am very fond of you and Alec, and the last thing I want is to see you suffer. But you're a grown woman—you're doing a master's for fuck's sake. I can't meddle in this romance any more than I already have. G'bye, my dear, and hope to see you soon."

There was a click, and I was alone in. Mrs. Barrymore's front room.

I stared dully at the church newsletter before me. It was two weeks old. I tore off the bit with the hotels' numbers and thrust it into my pocket.

Slowly, I ascended the stairs. I hardly knew what to do with the numbers or Lucas's theory.

His words had a certain point. What if I hadn't seen the start of an embrace, but simply Cheryl's attempt to initiate one? Should I at least call Alec at the hotel and demand an explanation?

But how? I could advise a hundred Mr. Pockmarks to get lost, but how would I begin this conversation with Alec? Tell him what I saw? Ask him what it meant? Demand to know why he didn't tell me about Cheryl in the first place?

And even if I liked his answers, it didn't mean he would be telling the truth.

Even if he loved me or said he did, it didn't mean he would pass up a chance with someone like Cheryl.

I felt the scrap of paper in my pocket and returned to my Royalist poets.

I thought about calling Liverpool that evening. For the next two days, I contemplated ringing Dublin.

I didn't.

Lila returned on Friday afternoon. She knocked tentatively on my bedroom door. "Would you like a cup of tea or something?"

"Yes, please."

A few minutes later, she carried two steaming mugs of tea into the room. She handed one to me and sat on the bed.

I inhaled the tea's aroma. There was something comforting about the steam and the ritual; no wonder the English were so attached to it.

"How was Bristol?" I asked.

"Good, thanks. I heard an excellent lecture about dating pigments." For a few minutes, we spoke of the lectures she had attended and the meals she'd had with Harry. Then she paused.

"Are you all right?" she asked quietly.

"You know then."

"Ravi took me aside pretty much as soon as I walked through the door."

"I'm okay. Perhaps it's all for the best."

She didn't probe or even look at me. She just sat sipping her tea and facing the wall, a kind, unobtrusive Egyptian queen in her flared jeans and black V-neck top, ready to hear anything I chose to reveal.

"It started on Sunday. When I went to Sheffield." And then, unprompted, the whole story tumbled out, concluding with Lucas's phone call two days earlier.

"And will you call?" she asked when I finished.

"I don't know. It would have to be today because it's their last night in Dublin. And maybe it's for the best."

"That they're leaving Dublin tomorrow morning?"

"No, that I've split up with Alec. If it's not Cheryl, it will be someone else." I paused. "A lot of someones."

"I can see that." But her assent was quiet.

The weekend arrived, and I didn't ring Dublin. I did survive a call from home.

"Mom, I've split up with Alec," I said after our initial greetings. Directness might deflect some awkward questions.

"I had a feeling I should call you," said my mom heavily. She often reported premonitions, and her intuition was usually right.

"Honey, are you okay?" she asked after a pause.

"I'm fine."

"Anything you want to tell me about?"

"No. Not now. But thank you."

We chatted cheerfully enough about family news. When she passed the phone to my dad, I heard loud whispering. My dad called me honey, and his gruff voice was uncharacteristically tender.

"You can't imagine how much your mother and I miss you," he said when we said goodbye.

I choked back tears.

Nana, too, had been briefed, for while there were the usual questions about my work at my university, there were none about Alec.

Maggie rang shortly after. I knew Mom had gotten to her, for she asked no awkward questions, answered mine gently, and said she loved me before we hung up.

I was lucky, really. People who couldn't really afford it had made transatlantic calls to tell me they loved me.

Mrs. Barrymore prided herself on her Sunday dinners, and that evening, she served roast beef with Yorkshire pudding and carrots.

"Have you got enough gravy, Miss Farrell?" she asked.

She was really trying. "Yes, I've got plenty, thank you. It's lovely."

The phone pealed from the front room. I started. Perhaps Lucas had spoken to Alec after all.

"I'll get it!" I said. I almost leapt from my seat and raced to the front room. Mrs. Barrymore might insist on fielding all calls, but I would answer this call from Alec.

"Hello?" I said when I picked up the receiver.

"Hello, may I please speak to Mr. Ravi Singh?" asked an Indian voice.

Of course, it wasn't Alec. I had been foolish to expect otherwise.

"Of course," I replied. "Who may I say is calling?"

"I am Rameesh Singh, brother of Mr. Ravi Singh. Do I have the honor of speaking with Mrs. Barrymore, my brother's gracious and esteemed landlady?"

I suppressed a giggle. He sounded like a caricature of an Indian.

"No, I'm one of the other lodgers. One moment, Mr. Singh."

Mrs. Barrymore glanced at me coldly when I returned to the dining room.

I nodded to Ravi. "For you, Mr. Singh."

He flashed his white teeth and bounded up to take his call.

The four of us ate in silence for a few minutes. I had irked Mrs. Barrymore by answering the phone. No more gravy for me.

A few minutes later, Ravi returned to his place.

"And who was that, Mr. Singh?" asked Mrs. Barrymore.

"My brother from New Delhi," replied Ravi.

Ralph frowned. "It's a funny time for him to be calling. Isn't it quite late in India?"

"That is very true, Mr. Taylor. But my brother had an important favor to ask of me."

All eyes were on him as he cut his meat.

"What's the favor?" asked Lila.

"He desires a bowler hat," he replied simply. "He believe it will make him one of the smartest men in New Delhi, and so he has charged me with acquiring one for him."

Mrs. Barrymore smiled. "That's lovely, sending a bit of civilization home to your brother. Mr. Taylor can help you find a nice one. He works with lawyers, so he'll know where they buy their hats."

Lila's eyes met mine over her glass. I swallowed my mouthful of carrots too quickly and coughed. Life might not hold grand passions or lasting love, but it might yield a bowler hat.

Twenty-Six

The next evening, Ralph invited us to join him and Miss Adams for tea the following Sunday.

"She's keen to meet all of you," he said. "We could meet at around noon after she's done teaching Sunday school."

Lila, Ravi, and I all murmured our assent. Lips pursed, Mrs. Barrymore drew herself up.

"Ralph, I would very much like to meet Miss Adams, but as you know, I'm occupied with the Sunday school at that hour."

The Church of England Sunday school warranted the definite article unlike its Methodist counterpart.

"Aunt Ann, I'm sorry—"

"No need to be. Why don't you invite Miss Adams to dinner one night the following week? It will be pleasant to have a nice young woman about the table."

Lila's eyes flitted to mine.

I was grateful to have this modest outing to look forward to. It would be a relief to meet someone who wouldn't ask me about Alec, and it would be interesting to meet Ralph's girlfriend.

That week, I ventured into the library for a few hours each day; I even had a tutorial with Timothy Burgess. But I kept my head down and walked quickly whenever I was on campus, and I avoided the English postgraduate office. While I would have welcomed Larry and Clara's camaraderie, I dreaded even their innocent inquiries, and I certainly didn't want to face Belle and Jules's pity and condescension.

On Sunday morning, Ravi and Lila gave their excuses; they were too preoccupied with work to have tea. And so Ralph and I walked to the center alone. We talked briefly about his work, and he spoke mostly about cars. He planned to purchase one soon, and he'd been researching his options.

Miss Adams awaited us outside Meng and Ecker. She wore a medium-length pale pink dress with a white cardigan, and a long light brown bob framed her dimpled cheeks. She smiled rather nervously when we shook hands.

"It's so lovely to meet you, Laura," I said when Ralph introduced us.

She giggled. "It's lovely to meet you."

Over tea and slices of madeira cake, we made conversation. At first, it was a struggle; Laura answered my questions about her work and home in monosyllables, punctuated with nervous giggles.

"How old are the children in your Sunday school class?" I asked finally.

"I have the infants—that is, the four and five-year-olds. They're very sweet."

If cars were the gateway to Ralph's heart, small children were the key to Laura's. We chatted easily for the rest of the outing with Laura relating anecdotes about her students and siblings, all of whom were younger than herself.

After tea, Ralph insisted on hailing a cab. The walk home would have been too much for Laura. When the driver stopped at Laura's house, he exited to kiss her goodbye at the doorway.

I smiled, averting my eyes from their embrace. They would make a lovely couple. Perhaps I should find someone like Ralph, a steady young man who would endow me with all sorts of virtues and kiss me tenderly.

"Laura seems lovely," I said when Ralph rejoined me in the cab. "She really opened up when I asked her about the Sunday school."

"Oh, Laura loves children. I can't imagine anyone better with them."

Ralph paused. "She was a bit nervous about meeting you at first, you know," he said finally.

"Really?" No one had ever found me intimidating before, but there was a first time for everything.

"Well, she knew you were American and doing a master's, and she knew you used to go out with a rock musician."

I absorbed the compliment. When it was put that way, I did sound rather impressive.

"So she imagined someone very clever and glamorous," Ralph continued. "Someone like Lila."

"Of course, you are clever," he added kindly.

On second thought, perhaps Miss Adams was not so lucky.

As the cab pulled into Mrs. Barrymore's street, I wondered where Alec was. Somewhere between Amsterdam and Stockholm if my memory served me well.

***

The following week, a note arrived from Mandy:

Dear Elsie,

I'm sorry I've not written sooner. I asked Dave to get your address from Alec, but he's got a memory like a sieve, and so it took a few reminders before he remembered.

I was sorry to hear about you and Alec. I wanted to ring when Dave told me the news, but I remembered that your landlady is a bit of a dragon, and I also thought you might like some space.

In any case, I really enjoyed our outing in London. Do hope you'd like to do it again sometime. Or it'd be lovely to have you at ours for dinner. Dave and I mean to give some dinner parties, and you could meet our cat, Butler. Dave's not a cat person, but Butler's brought him round.

Ring me!

Much love,

Mandy

I looked out the window onto the street. I tried to imagine myself sitting opposite Dave and Mandy, eating prawns and pasta and bantering over cocktails. I couldn't.

I would ring Mandy, but not yet.

***

A couple Sundays later, my mom called in the afternoon. "How are you, Elsie honey?" she asked. Her voice was warm, but hurried.

"All right."

Something banged on her end.

"Are you cooking, Mom?"

"No. Why do you ask?"

"It sounds like someone's banging pots and pans over there."

"No, we're just getting ready to go to a ball game."

That wasn't like my parents at all. They were avid baseball fans, but they were usually content to watch the Yankees on television or to listen to games on the radio.

"A Yankee game?"

"No, the Mets. They're playing the Dodgers."

It didn't make sense. "But you and Dad hate the Mets."

"Your brother-in-law got tickets."

Once again, I heard clanging.

"Mom, is this a good time for you to talk?"

"It's fine. Oh, your father wants to talk to you. Love you, honey."

In rapid succession, Dad and Nana told me they loved me. Then they said goodbye.

Shaking my head, I replaced the phone in the receiver. None of it made sense. My parents and Nana were ardent Yankee fans, they always teased Maggie's husband George about being a Mets fan, and my dad had never forgiven the Dodgers for deserting Brooklyn for Los Angeles in the fifties.

It was hard to imagine them at a Mets-Dodgers game even if George had tickets.

Above all, I was a little hurt. I looked forward to their monthly calls, and there was so much I wanted to ask them about, the animals, Dad's work, Maggie's family, and Mom's books. And I'd been looking forward to telling them about Ravi's quest for a bowler hat and my progress on my dissertation.

And although we would exchange letters, it would be another month before I would hear their voices again.

***

The next day, I braved the English postgraduate office. Larry and Clara greeted me warmly, and even Belle and Jules summoned airy helloes from the loveseat in the corner.

"I've not seen you in ages, pet," said Clara. "Think it's been a month! Of course, I've been in my own dissertation mousehole in the library, so that's partially my fault."

"I've been buried in books as well," I said.

Over a cup of tea, the three of us chatted about our dissertations. Then the conversation veered into more personal channels. I asked Larry about Sally, and he, of course, inquired about Alec.

"Is Alec still on tour?" he asked.

I was ready. "Yes, " I replied. "But we're not together anymore."

Larry's blue eyes were concerned. "You all right, Elsie?"

"Oh, my God, pet, I had no idea," said Clara. "I'm so sorry."

"It's been about a month," I said evenly. "It's fine. Now."

"Oh, too bad, Elsie," said Jules lazily, putting an arm around Belle's shoulders.

"It happens," sighed Belle as if rain had stalled a child's picnic.

I chose to ignore them.

"How is Angie?" I asked Clara.

"I don't know, pet. It's funny that we've both been hiding away for the past month since that's how long it's been since I talked to Angie."

So I hadn't been alone in my heartache. "I'm so sorry—"

She shook her head. "It's all right. She wouldn't tell her mum about us, and I haven't called her since."

For a moment, the postgraduate office was silent. Even Belle and Jules had the decency to shut up. Then Larry cleared his throat.

"Rogers and I have been thinking we ought to have a dinner party. Just a few people round for food and plonk. Be good to see both of you."

We agreed it would be lovely, and I wondered why I had avoided my friends for so long.

That afternoon, before walking home, I ventured into the center. Lila and I had talked of going to the seaside, and I decided to look at bathing suits at Dorothy Perkins. I hadn't brought mine from home, and I wanted something relatively inexpensive.

On my way into the shop, I passed a woman heading out. There was something familiar about her thin face.

"Angie?" I asked tentatively.

She almost jumped.

"I'm Elsie," I said. "We met a couple times this winter." I didn't want to mention that I was on Clara's course.

Her features softened into a smile. "Of course, I remember you. You all right?"

"For the most part. Busy with my dissertation."

She looked down. It was impossible to discuss my course without reminding her of Clara.

We talked briefly about her work as a nurse. She had been moved to the pediatric ward.

"It's hard," she said. "You get attached to the kids, but I wouldn't have it any other way."

I saw the kindness in her eyes and knew she would be a great nurse. I also saw the capacity for pain.

"Angie," I said slowly. "I don't like to meddle—"

"Yes?" Her hazel eyes searched my face eagerly. She was positively asking me to interfere. I remember how I had entreated Lucas to speak to Alec for me.

"I think—I think you should call Clara. I think she regrets it."

For a moment, Angie stared at me. Then, a smile illuminated her angular features.

"Thank you," she said quietly and hurried out of the shop.

What if Clara spurned her? I hoped I had done the right thing.

I found a modest one-piece blue swimsuit. It was hardly fit for a rock star's girlfriend, but I no longer was one, and I suppose I had broken the mold anyway.

Slowly, I walked home from the center. When I entered the foyer, Mrs. Barrymore was muttering in the kitchen.

"I let one of them into my house, but are they content with that?" she asked. "No, now there are three, and who knows how many more may descend on me before it's all said and done?"

I frowned. Ravi must have relations visiting. Strange that he'd not mentioned it. But that tirade wasn't like Mrs. Barrymore at all. She was normally delighted to demonstrate that she harbored no prejudice against South Asians.

I decided to say hello. If Ravi's relatives had any knowledge of English, they would get the gist of her soliloquy, and I wanted them to experience a little civility during their time in Manchester.

Tentatively, I opened the door.

But the faces that greeted me were not Indian. Two white women, one plump and middle-aged with soft brown hair and the other older and thin with short chestnut hair, occupied Mrs. Barrymore's green sofa. When I entered the room, they stood up in unison.

"Hi, honey!" cried the plump one.

"Hello, dear," said the slender one.

"Mom, Nana," I said, hugging both of them in turn. "How did you get here?"

"We took a plane, of course," replied Nana. "From New York to London."

"And that nice Irishman drove us to Manchester today," said Mom. "Oh, it's so good to see you, Elsie." Once again, she drew me into her soft embrace. She smelled faintly of the Chanel No. 5 perfume she kept for special occasions.

My mother and grandmother in Mrs. Barrymore's front room. It was a dream in which everything was wonderful and nothing made sense.

"What Irishman?" I demanded. "And where's Dad? Is everything all right?" Suddenly, I panicked. Had they come to Manchester to tell me something had happened at the Mets game?

"His name was Sean," said Nana. "He was very large, but very polite."

"And your father's fine," replied my mom in a soothing tone. "He's having a beer with Alec."

Twenty-Seven

"What?" I shrieked. "I didn't know about this."

"Well, you weren't supposed to, dear," replied Nana evenly. "It was a surprise for you."

I almost fell into Mrs. Barrymore's green chair. "I meant Alec."

"He's the reason we're here," said Mom.

"But we're not together anymore."

"He still wanted you to see us."

I sank further into the green chair. None of it made any sense.

After a few more exchanges like this, the truth emerged. Alec had called my parents a couple weeks earlier. He had offered to fly them to England and pay their hotel fare for a week.

"He would have flown your sister and her family over, but Maggie thought Patrick was too young to fly," said Nana. "And George had to work, of course."

"And he even offered to compensate your father for the time he'd have to take off work," added Mom. "Of course, he said no—you know your father has a lot of pride."

"I'm surprised he let Alec pay for the plane tickets," I said dully. It didn't sound like my dad at all. He barely allowed people to buy him a hamburger.

"I think Alec said something that really touched your father; they hit it off right away."

Dad and Alec had hit it off. It was surreal, but then again, so were Mom and Nana in Mrs. Barrymore's front room.

"You—you've met Alec?"

"Oh, we just said hello when he came by about an hour ago. He's just come back from Rome, you know."

Only I didn't. But now that I thought of it, I recalled the tour was concluding in Italy.

My mind scampered. Did this mean Alec wanted to make amends? But if that was the case, why hadn't he called or written from the road? None of it made sense.

"So how long have you been here?" I asked. "Has Mrs. Barrymore made you comfortable?"

"She is a very dignified lady," replied Nana. Her blue eyes were wide behind her glasses. "She has excellent posture, and she calls us Mrs. Farrell and Mrs. Hayes. She has a kind heart, though; she brought us tea and an ashtray."

My mom made a face that told me the rest of the story.

I asked them questions about their trip and tried not to think about Alec. Sean, Serval's enormous Irish roadie, had met them at Heathrow the previous evening and brought them to their hotel. This morning, he'd driven them to Manchester. They'd been at Mrs. Barrymore's house for about two hours.

"He pointed out some of the sights, but said we would have a proper tour later," said Mom. "If you can take a break from school, he'll drive us to London for a few days."

"Yes, of course." I tried to smile. I was torn between jubilation that they were in England and bewilderment about the circumstances that brought them there.

Outside, a car stopped. From the window, I saw Alec's blue Mercedes on the opposite side of the street. My dad sat in the front seat beside Alec. They shook hands, Dad exited the car, and Alec drove away.

I had been foolish to expect otherwise.

I raced to the front door and summoned a hug for my dad. When his blue eyes smiled into mine and he enfolded me in his arms, tears formed in my eyes.

"Good to see you, honey," he said.

For a few minutes, the four of us chatted in Mrs. Barrymore's front room. Then he cleared his throat.

"In an hour, Sean is coming to take us to dinner. My treat. Then he'll drive your mother and Nana and me to our bed-and-breakfast. But first, there's a letter for you."

He withdrew an envelope from his back pocket and handed it to me. "You might want to be alone when you read it."

For a gruff guy, Dad could be tactful. I nodded mutely and raced up the stairs.

Once I was safe inside my room, I opened the letter. The firm, clear handwriting was familiar.

June 1973

Elsie,

About a week after our last call, Lucas took me aside and told me the truth. I realized I owed you an apology and an explanation, and this letter is an attempt at both.

I was wrong not to tell you about my past relationship with Cheryl. I know that now. It was sheer cowardice, and there's no excuse for it. I didn't want to upset you or provoke a scene at Mike's party, so I pretended there had never been anything between Cheryl and me. The band, their wives, and the crew played along. In retrospect, I ought to have known you would find out somehow.

Cheryl and I were together about a year. Initially, I found her enchanting. One minute, she was assured and flirtatious, the next a needy little girl. Her background was difficult, and I found myself wanting to take care of her.

She made excuses for her behavior, and I believed them. She berated a backup singer in front of her band because touring was particularly hard for her. She couldn't attend my dad's funeral because it would have brought up unpleasant memories from her past.

She brought two different men, one of whom was the tennis announcer you met at Mike's party, to my house whilst I was away because she felt lonely and neglected when I was touring and then when I was at my dad's funeral. There was a big row when I found out, but she cried and seemed so contrite that I forgave her willingly.

And I was far from perfect. There are always temptations in my business, and one night in Upsala last September, I succumbed. She must have had her spies amongst the crew because she rang me at our hotel in Helsinki. She called from her flat in Belgravia, but she announced that she was going to drive to Kent, remove all my remaining guitars from the house, and make a bonfire of them in the back garden.

Fortunately, I was able to reach Mrs. Hall. She and Jim were able to summon a locksmith to change all the locks before Cheryl arrived. For arrive she did. I've no idea whether she came armed with petrol, but she did drive to my house and kick at the doors. Then she tore across the street to the Halls' house, where she raved outside their front door for three-quarters of an hour. She was lucky that Jim prevailed; Mrs. Hall would have rung the police.

But even after that, I decided to try again. We agreed that the only solution was to go on tour together. I had a couple gigs in the early winter I couldn't change, but we arranged for her to tour with Serval the following spring.

Christmas came. I wanted to see my mother, but Cheryl wouldn't accompany me. Her family was unhappy, so no one else was to be happy with their relations. I would have just spent one day with my mum in Yorkshire by myself, but even that was too much for Cheryl. She needed a holiday in the sun, and so we spent Christmas in Tenerife.

She allowed me to ring my mum on Christmas Day, and I agreed to talk for no more than a quarter of an hour while she had a drink in the bar. But Mum was clearly so grateful for that call that I ended up talking to her for nearly forty-five minutes. When I returned to the bar, Cheryl was livid. In front of the barkeep, she accused me of cruelty and desertion and brought up my lapse in Sweden because I had talked too long to my widowed mother on Christmas Day.

She exhausted herself screaming, and then, back in the room, she laid down on the bed, crying. I slunk off back to the hotel's bar. About three-quarters of the way through a bottle of cheap Spanish wine, I realized it was Christmas. Other people were opening crackers and enjoying themselves with their families. I wondered how many Christmases I wanted to spend drowning my sorrows in an empty bar.

And so I bid adieu to Cheryl and checked into another hotel. It was the only one I could find at that hour on Christmas night, and it was filthy, but I was free. I flew home the next day. As a parting gift, Cheryl sent me a telegram announcing that she'd bedded one of the hotel's porters.

Then, one night in January, I met you. My intentions were strictly dishonorable when we began, but that changed quickly. You were clever and funny and beautiful and adorable, and I fell in love with you. I hope you know that.

Serval went on tour with Cheryl because of a prior agreement. We had no way of getting out of it though the whole band dearly wanted to. I decided to make the best of it. I would treat her with businesslike friendliness and keep my distance.

She saw my stance as a challenge. She was always trying to corral me into having meals or drinks with her. Sometimes, I made excuses; at others, I ensured we had a group outing. And sometimes, I simply avoided her.

Things came to a head after our show in Sheffield. She attempted to embrace me outside the band's dressing room. You witnessed that. What you didn't see was me removing Cheryl's hands from my shoulders. I told her I was with you and I loved you, and I wished her the best.

And from then on, I ensured we stayed at different hotels. It was an inconvenience since it meant I was separated from the rest of the band and crew, but it was worth it.

Above all, I'm sorry. Had I been honest with you, I might have spared you some pain. And perhaps we might still be together.

After the tour, I'd planned to bring your family over to England for a visit. Since you'd given me back my family, I wanted to do something similar for you. As it was, I had to resort to surreptitious methods to get your parents' number. They seem lovely by the way.

I am sorry I hurt you, and I thank you for the time we had together. I have no right to demand anything further from you, but I wish you all the best with your studies and career. I remain

Yours Ever,

Alec

I gulped. Only he wasn't mine. The letter had told everything and changed nothing.

Twenty-Eight

The four of us had dinner at the King's Arms. Dad wanted to try fish and chips, Mom and Nana were eager to sample pub fare, and since Lila and I occasionally ate there, I knew we could get a good meal.

"This is very cozy," said Mom as we slid into a high-backed booth.

"So, how was the Mets game?" I asked.

My parents looked at each other and burst out laughing.

"There never was a Mets game, honey," said Dad. "Well, there was, but we didn't go."

"So you made that up? To throw me off the scent?"

My mom grinned. "You got it. Could you see your father and me at a Mets game of all things? It'd be like changing our religion!"

"That's reassuring. But why did you call? If you couldn't really talk."

"We wanted to say goodbye to you before we left, dear," said Nana.

They had questions about my dissertation and my friends and my house. I answered them as cheerfully as I could and inquired about their flight and their hotel. Alec had put them up at a small bed-and-breakfast near the university.

Alec had made the right decision. They would never have felt comfortable at the Midland or the Piccadilly, and this way, Dad wouldn't feel too beholden to Alec.

Though it was wonderful to see them and hear their voices, my mind kept wandering to Alec's letter.

After a leisurely dinner, Sean ferried my parents and Nana to their bed-and-breakfast. The plan was that they'd sleep late, I'd go to uni in the morning, and then we'd explore Manchester in the afternoon. The next day, we'd leave for London.

I went to bed in a daze, and although I slept deeply, I awoke in the same state the next morning. At breakfast, I could barely answer Ravi's cheerful inquiries about my plans with my family.

Lila wasn't going to campus that day, so I walked alone to uni in the same trance. When I approached the library, I realized I was about as ready to research Royalist poets as I was to perform brain surgery. I veered off to the Arts Building. Perhaps a cup of tea would snap me out of it. Whatever it was.

Jules and Belle were the only people in the postgrad office. As usual, they occupied the loveseat in the corner. Jules held a ream of paper, presumably his dissertation on freedom in post-war fiction, Belle a hand-rolled cigarette. I should have guessed it. Larry and Clara never made an appearance until the afternoon.

"Hello, Elsie," said Jules. He even made a simple greeting sound condescending. Once his tone would have annoyed me. Now I didn't care.

"Hi," I replied absently.

Belle tittered. "You sound faraway, Elsie. Almost as though you were speaking from the seventeenth century."

"Well, I have been immersing myself in the era."

"That must be a lovely escape—after your disappointment."

It was a low blow even for her. I chose to ignore it. "I'm making a pot of tea. Would either of you like some?"

"No, thanks," replied Jules.

"I'm all right," said Belle.

I filled the kettle. I would drink my tea and leave. Even in my vague state, Jules and Belle were insupportable.

"I wouldn't mind a cuppa," said a northern voice. "If there's enough in the kettle."

I swung around. In flared jeans and a white t-shirt, Alec stood in the doorway.

He smiled, but there was something in his eyes I hadn't seen before. Hesitation, perhaps.

"Don't mind Elsie, she can't speak today," said Belle.

"There's enough water," I replied.

"But maybe a walk first," said Alec.

I nodded mutely and shut off the kettle. Silently, we walked downstairs and onto the grass outside the building. Alec's dark eyes blinked in the sun.

"Thank you for bringing my family to me," I said. It seemed inadequate after all that had passed.

"My pleasure." He stuck his hands in his pockets. "Elsie, you've heard—that is, you've read—my story by now."

I nodded.

"I'm sorry for everything. And after all I've put you through, the last thing I want to do is bother you. If you tell me to leave, I'll bugger off and never bother you again. So, Elsie, do I stay or do I go?"

"Please stay." My voice broke.

"Elsie." He drew me close, and his lean arms were around me. I hadn't dared to hope I would ever feel his arms around me or smell him again.

"Then I have one more question for you," he said. His mouth was very close to my ear. I was dimly aware that people were passing us on all sides, walking toward the library and the refractory, but they seemed far away.

"Yes?" My voice was small. Perhaps he was going to ask me where I wanted to go for dinner.

Suddenly, he knelt in front of me. "Will you marry me?"

"Yes!" I squeaked.

Then he was on his feet, and I was in his arms, and his mouth was on mine.

When we parted, his velvety eyes smiled into mine, and we kissed all over again.

Then I pulled away. "One thing's bothering me: how did you get my parents' number?"

"That was easy. Ravi gave it to me."

"Ravi? I don't remember you calling Ravi."

Alec grinned. "No, but Rameesh Singh did," he said in an Indian accent.

"That was you? No wonder I wanted to laugh. You sounded like a cartoon Indian."

"And here I was flattering myself that I'd managed a credible accent."

We laughed, and he kissed me again. I'd never dared to hope I could be this happy.

I was still laughing when we pulled apart. My eyes strayed to the Arts Building Extension. Eyes wide, two faces were pressed to a third-floor window.

I waved merrily to Belle and Jules and wished they would be as happy as I was.

Twenty-Nine

That afternoon, Alec drove my family around Manchester, and we showed them some of the sights. Because of our engagement, we modified our plans for the following week. Since my mom had read a number of novels set in Yorkshire and expressed a desire to see that part of the country, Alec offered to drive us to Yorkshire for a couple days. Ruth had been ecstatic when she'd heard of our engagement, and she'd invited all of us to have lunch at her cottage. After our visit to Yorkshire, we'd drive down to London for a few days of proper sightseeing before my parents and Nana flew back to the States.

But the day after Alec proposed, we had an engagement party at Isola Bella. First, Alec ferried Lila, Ravi, and Mrs. Barrymore to Isola Bella before returning to pick up my family. Ralph was bringing Laura in the 1968 Ford Cortina he'd just purchased. It was light blue, and I was happy to note that it looked a lot like Alec's Mercedes.

Nana answered the door when Alec arrived at the house to collect us. "Hello, Alec," she said with a smile.

"Good evening, Mrs. Hayes—wow!"

I was descending the stairs in my blue dress and a pair of white heeled sandals. Alec's velvety eyes smiled into mine.

Nana laughed merrily.

"You have a beautiful granddaughter, Mrs. Hayes."

"We are very proud of her."

Then I remembered Mandy and felt a pang. She had wanted to be there when Alec saw me in the dress. I would ring her the following week.

"How did you manage to reserve the entire restaurant?" my dad asked as Alec parked opposite Isola Bella.

Alec grinned at him in the rearview mirror. "It was easy. Only one couple had reservations, and when Mr. Barbieri told them their next dinner was paid for, they were happy to change their plans."

Mr. Barbieri himself greeted us. He smiled broadly when we entered the restaurant's foyer. "Congratulations, Mr. Wilder, on winning the hand of such a bella donna."

Next, the proprietor fussed around Mom and Nana. "Good evening, Mrs. Hayes, Mrs. Farrell. Let me take your coats."

My mom's green eyes were wide as he removed her jacket. Nana, I noticed, stood a little taller. She'd left school when she was thirteen to work in a laundry, and she had never imagined a time when she might be an honored guest at a decent restaurant.

The staff had pushed together several tables to create one long one. Members of our party stood about chatting in small groups. Larry and Sally approached us. They kissed my cheek, and Larry shook Alec's hand.

"So happy for you, Elsie. Congratulations, Alec."

"Thanks, mate. Good to see you tonight."

There were voices in the foyer. I turned to see Clara and Angie enter the room hand in hand.

"You're together!" I said.

"I might say the same to you and Alec, pet," replied Clara. "And I understand I owe you a drink or two or three. Congratulations, Alec. You are a lucky man."

"Don't I know it." Alec kissed my forehead.

I hugged both girls in turn. "Thanks," Angie whispered in my ear.

In this case, my meddling had paid off.

Mr. Barbieri appeared with something small in his hand. "A telegram for the happy couple."

Alec opened the message, and I read it over his shoulder.

"Congratulations Alec and love to Elsie STOP Pam and I look forward to celebrating soon STOP Lucas STOP."

Alec folded the telegram and placed it in his wallet. "I haven't told the rest of the band or crew, but I thought you wouldn't mind if I rang Lucas."

"I should think not; he was there from the beginning." And, in some measure, he was the reason we were there tonight.

A few waiters appeared to take our orders, and our party arranged itself around the long table. I sat beside Alec, of course, while Ravi sat on his other side and Lila next to me.

""Aunt Harriet" sends her regrets," said Lila. "But she hopes both of you will come to Bristol soon."

"It's about time we met," I said. "I just hope she won't be too disapproving."

Next, I addressed Ravi. "So I understand I have you to thank for all of this."

He grinned. "You are very gracious, Elsie, but it is Alec who reserved the restaurant."

"I meant for my family's visit—and for the fact that Alec is here."

"I helped, yes."

"But how did you get my parents' number for Alec?"

Ravi's smile broadened. "It was a simple matter of entering your room and ensuring that the intrusion escaped both your notice and that of our esteemed landlady. So, a few Sundays ago, when Mrs. Barrymore was busy with the Sunday school and you were enjoying tea with Ralph and Laura, Lila entered your room and removed the address book from your desk. As a skilled Egyptologist, she is very attentive to detail, and so she was able to remove and replace it without attracting your notice."

"Did you?" I asked Lila.

Her grey eyes glinted. "I might have done."

Alec was grinning. "Did you know anything about this?" I demanded.

"All I did was ring Ravi. He sorted it out from there."

Then Mr. Barbieri, flanked by two waiters, arrived with bottles of champagne. Once every glass was poured, Alec stood up.

"Two toasts," he said, sounding oddly shy.

"First, to my Elsie. She's got beauty and brains, she's the sweetest girl I've ever met, and somehow she agreed to become my missus."

"To Elsie!" Everyone raised their glasses and took a sip. Even the abstemious Mrs. Barrymore drank to our future happiness.

Alec raised his glass again. "And to meddlers. Those who are here and those who couldn't be here tonight. Without them, I wouldn't be where I am today."

"Here, here," said Clara.

We raised our glasses and drank again.

Then the waiters brought baskets of crusty bread, and there was a murmur of conversation around the table.

Nana and Mrs. Barrymore sat kitty-corner to us. Since discovering that she would not be responsible for putting up my family, Mrs. Barrymore had become more hospitable. In Nana, she hoped she might have found a moral ally, albeit a Catholic and American one.

"Did you see those two young women, Mrs. Hayes? They came in holding hands."

Nana's blue eyes were large behind her glasses. "Yes, but I think they are nice girls, Mrs. Barrymore," she replied. "The one with short hair is a good friend of Elsa's, and the other one is a nurse. She takes care of sick children."

Mrs. Barrymore sniffed. "That's as may be, Mrs. Hayes, but it's not natural, is it?"

"God made all people," Nana murmured.

There was no way even Mrs. Barrymore could dispute this theological point.

"So what do you think of Mr. Wilder?" asked Mrs. Barrymore.

"He has long hair and plays loud music, but he has a kind heart," replied Nana. "He took us around Manchester, and next he will take us sightseeing in Yorkshire and London."

Mrs. Barrymore inclined her head. "On the whole, Mrs. Hayes, I agree with you."

I caught Alec's eyes, and we had a private smile in the middle of the noisy room.

Alec's mouth was close to my ear. "What are you thinking, Elsie?"

"Lots of things," I replied. "Like what we should name our first cat."

"And what did you have in mind?"

"How about Lynx?" I asked.

Acknowledgements

It takes a village to raise a child, and any serious author quickly discovers that it requires a small battalion to bring a book to fruition.

Although the 1970s are within living memory, it proved a surprisingly challenging era to resurrect. So much about our daily life has changed in the past fifty years, and even people who remember that decade struggle to recall these details. Whilst writing *Elsie and the Lynx*, I had to research minutia as far flung as cat rescue and Easter chocolate. During this journey, I was privileged to encounter so many helpful and diligent archivists who cheerfully answered my inquiries about these topics. I am grateful to, in alphabetical order, Sophie Clapp at Boots Archive, Kethi Copeland Nuttall at the City of Westminster Archive, James Peters at the University of Manchester Library, Tom Richardson at the North Yorkshire County Record Office, and Francesca Watson at Cats Protection. Sarah at Betty's Café and Sebastian at the Harrods Company Archive proved equally obliging although I never learned their surnames.

While archival research is exciting, nothing replaces the thrill of the personal interview. I am indebted to Angela Sherlock, Naomi Mattingly, and especially Sarah McCartney for answering my relentless questions about life in 1970s Britain. Sarah, I am, as ever, astounded by your ability to field inquiries about furniture, florists, and band security. If you should ever tire of your brain, please loan it to me. Richard Rooks, thank you for so generously sharing your memories, snapshots, and encyclopedic collection of 1970s catalogues and magazines with me. You not only enlightened me about Biba, Pan's People, and *Top of the Pops*, but provided much-needed encouragement during the project's early stages. On the other side of the Atlantic, Dolores Dahm set me straight on Jersey City in the 1970s.

One of the joys of independent publishing is assembling one's own dream team of colleagues. I am honored to have worked with the eagle-eyed Molly Spain. Those of us with advanced degrees in writing and literature think we are skilled proofreaders until we attempt to proofread our own writing. Carolyn Dahm suggested a fetching URL, and Paul Dahm gave me a more attractive website than I could have imagined. I suspect the world doesn't hold enough wine or chocolate to repay him for his labors. From down under, Shirley Tran provided stunning typography and cover layout. Finally, I was fortunate to have enlisted an illustrator of Simon Reid's caliber, let alone one as preoccupied with cats and rock musicians as I am, to bring my characters to life. I damn well hope this book lives up to its cover.

I am also grateful to those individuals who, directly or indirectly, made the manuscript what is today. The anonymous judges in the New Jersey Romance Writers Put Your Heart in a Book Contest helped me strengthen the narrative and refine Elsie's voice. While editing the novel, I benefited from the New England Romance Writers' excellent monthly workshops about all aspects of craft. In addition, my critique group, Bliss Bennet, A. G. Meyers, Karen Kaletka, and Tricia. L. Woods, offered trenchant feedback about the book's first couple chapters. Above all, I am grateful to the book's early readers, Lisa Hedicker, Emily Juniper, Thomas G.J. Sharpe, and especially Dolores Dahm and Colleen McMahon, who know how to boost a writer's confidence! Thanks for your love and encouragement and for your sincere pleasure in Elsie's story.

About the Author

Dora Campbell writes romances with wry heroines, roguish heroes, and imperfect but, she hopes, perfectly satisfying happily-ever-afters. When Dora's not writing, she's reading about British history, volunteering at her local animal shelter, or indulging in dark chocolate. She shares a Vermont farmhouse with a squeaky torbie cat. Visit her at https://doracampbell.ink.